PENGUIN BOOKS
The Dream Sleepers

Patricia Grace was born in Wellington in 1937. She is of Ngati Raukawa, Ngati Toa and Te Ati Awa descent, and is affiliated to Ngati Porou by marriage. She has taught in primary and secondary schools in the King Country, Northland and Porirua, where she now lives. She is married with seven children.

Patricia Grace's stories have been published in a number of periodicals and anthologies. Her first collection of stories, *Waiariki*, was published in 1975 (the first collection of stories by a Maori woman writer), and a second collection, *The Dream Sleepers*, in 1980. Her first novel, *Mutuwhenua, The Moon Sleeps*, was published in 1978. She has also written two children's books in English and Maori, illustrated by Robyn Kahukiwa, *The Kuia and the Spider* (1981) and *Watercress Tuna and the Children of Champion Street* (1985), the former winning the Children's Picture Book of the Year award in 1982. She also wrote the text for *Wahine Toa* (1984), illustrated by Robyn Kahukiwa.

In 1985 Patricia Grace was the Writing Fellow at Victoria University of Wellington.

Patricia Grace

The Dream Sleepers

PENGUIN BOOKS

Penguin Books (N.Z.) Ltd, 182–190 Wairau Road,
Auckland 10, New Zealand

Penguin Books Ltd, Harmondsworth,
Middlesex, England

Penguin Books, 40 West 23rd Street,
New York, N.Y.10010, U.S.A.

Penguin Books Australia Ltd, Ringwood,
Victoria, Australia

Penguin Books Canada Limited, 2801 John Street,
Markham, Ontario, Canada L3R 1B4

First published by Longman Paul Ltd 1980
Reprinted 1982
Published in Penguin Books 1986

Copyright © Patricia Grace 1980

Printed in Hong Kong

To the memory of Hurumutu Ropata

Contents

One

The Dream Sleepers

The houses sit on their handkerchiefs, and early in the morning begin to sneeze. They do not sneeze in unison but one at at time, or sometimes in pairs or threes, sometimes in tens or dozens. The footpaths and roads beyond the borders of the handkerchiefs quicken with the aftermath of sneezing.

The very earliest were the silent ones, quiet light tracing their movements from bedrooms, past sleepers who had not yet begun to dream their waking-up dreams, to bathrooms, to kitchens. The lights went out behind them, noiseless doors shut as they made their ways to the pick-up points, or got into taxis that would take them to the trains.

Juliet's mother was one of the three o'clockers. She hoped Bill would hear the alarm at six, and that Juliet would be ready for school and have breakfast ready by the time she got back at eight. Francie's grandmother was one, she hoped they would all get the jobs done quickly at work this morning, and that Elaine would empty the Hoover and wipe the chair legs without being told. Junior's sister was one, and she wanted someone she didn't yet know, to love her.

Juliet's mother and Francie's grandmother knotted their headscarves under their chins, turned their jacket collars up and walked together to the pick-up point. Junior's sister hurried to catch up to them thinking that they were old women and that they sometimes told her not to go on her own down the subway. But she enjoyed sitting in the van with them smoking, and listening to them have the driver on. Their gossip was good, and if she had a party she would invite them to it.

The five o'clockers were the next ones, a little less silent, putting lights on and off and turning on music. Putting the jug on and heating up food if there was time. But still, the sleepers, the ones who would eventually get to dreaming, had not yet arrived at that time. Some of the babies were awake already, mewing for food and dry clothes.

Neville woke his mother and put the baby's bottle in the jug to warm before he left for the delivery round. Dean's sister walked to the mall dairy where she made sandwiches until seven, and Pele's brother met Neville at the bus stop and they ran together to the corner where they could see the truck already on its way up the hill.

At seven the dream sleepers began flickering their eyelids, but the eight o'clock starters were already out on the footpaths, or in cars or buses. The lights of the street had just gone out.

At eight Juliet poured tea for her mother then went into the bedroom where she tied her cardigan round her waist making a large knot on her stomach with the ends of the sleeves, and letting the rest hang down like an apron over her backside. She toed her way into a pair of jandals and went across to meet Francie.

Francie was wearing a denim cap that she had snatched from Pele the day before. Her grandmother was seeing them all off to school before going back to bed, and her father had just got up for ten o'clock start. She and Juliet went to the dairy for chippies and gum.

Pele wanted the hat back but not because it was his.

He had pulled the hat from Junior's pocket earlier in the week, and now he needed it to cover up his haircut. He sat on the footpath to wait for Francie, or someone with a hat. He could see Neville and Dean coming and they were going to be smart about his hair. They were pushing Valerie to school in her wheelchair.

'Hey you Pele, you got a kina.'

'Who said?'

'Man I can see. I got eyes.'

'So what?'

'So you got a kina Pele boy.'

'Smart you. Fif formers.'

A dog came to sniff at him so he sat it down by him to wait. He hoped Francie and Juliet hadn't gone past already, but he thought they would be at the shops buying chippies and chewing gum. There were kids everywhere, and dogs. His dog ran away to watch a fight. It stood in the middle of the road with its ears up; a bus nosed up to it so it sidled away.

'Francie, Francie. Give us the hat.'

'Nah. It's not yours Pele.'

'Give it Francie.'

'Do you want some chippies Pele?'

'No I want the hat.'

'What for?'

'I want it.'

'Who gave you the kina Pele?'

'My sister, so what?'

'So take the hat then.'

'I got some smokes Francie.'

'Any matches?'

'We can run after Junior for some matches.'

'So a business letter is more formal isn't it, than a letter to a friend? What do you think that word means—

''formal''? If you got an invitation to a ball or something and your invitation said ''Dress formal'', how
would you dress?'

'Dress up.'

'Yes?'

'Dress up in your good things.'

'Right. How would the boys dress?'

'Suits and all that.'

'Ties.'

'Like poofters.'

'Church clothes.'

'Hair cut like Pele. Hey Pele you sucker.'

'O.K. What about the girls?'

'Long skirts and . . . .'

'Beads and that.'

'And platforms and fur coats.'

'All right. What about ''informal''?'

'Jeans and jandals.'

'Tee shirts.'

'Good, you've got the idea. Now about letters. Last
week we did the sort of letter you would write to a
friend — an informal letter. Now today . . . .'

Today there were concrete block walls and holes in
the lino just as there had been the day before. Sparrows
had been in shitting on the ledges and there was a door
somewhere that kept slamming. Va was passing spark-
les to Nga, and Peter had nearly finished drawing the
snake that coiled round and round from the back of his
hand to his elbow. There was an old moustache on the
poster of Elvis but the blacked-out tooth was new and
so were the pencil holes in the eyes.

'So there you are. Your address, top right-hand corner. Business address — ''The Personnel Officer, New
World Supermarket'', etcetera — below on the left . . . .'

'Buy a bigga blocka cheese . . . .'

'Then below that, "Dear Sir" . . . .'

'How a-are ya?'

'Then you start . . . .'

'I'm all ri-ight.'

'All right, no more nonsense, get on with it. Pele you shouldn't be wearing that hat in class should you?'

'Sir he can't help it his sister gave him a Kojak.'

'There's still plenty of hair on his head.'

'She gave him a kina.'

'All right, come on now, you've got fifteen minutes before lunch. I'll come round and help anyone who needs it.'

('Dear Sir, I am a fourteen-year-old girl and I would like . . . *to be allowed down to the town centre on late shopping nights.*'

'I saw your advertisement in the paper . . . *and today is like yesterday.*'

'I am reliable and I work hard and I . . . *can sing and dance.*'

'I am a boy aged fourteen . . . *and for lunch I'll buy two doughnuts, a coffee bun, and a Coke.*'

'I would like a job for the holidays . . . *and my mother will die soon.*'

'I can come to an interview . . . . *Then she walked*
away
Quietly so afraid
Smiling
But no doubt
Crying
Her   heart   out
. . . .'

'Yours faithfully . . . . *Crying*
Her heart out.

She really just wants
To stay . . . .')

'The bell Sir.'

'I know.'

'We don't want to be last down the canteen.'

'I've got to go home and put the meat in . . . .'

'All right, we'll have a look at those again tomorrow.'

Tomorrow there would be corridors to walk and steps to go down just as there were today. There'd be a group in the courtyard playing kick square, someone walking on the roof, and people waiting in rows in the canteen. There'd be more pie and doughnut bags to step on or over, and there'd be a swing door somewhere slamming back and forth. There'd be another message or two to read on the concrete block walls, and perhaps one to write. There was one to be written if only you could know what it was.

'So now just copy down that section into your books where it says "Our Heritage", showing all the things that have been handed down to us by the people of Ancient Greece, on page sixteen.'

'What for?'

'Why do we have to copy it down?'

'Who's that calling out? Page sixteen — if you work quickly and quietly you'll get it finished by the time the bell goes.'

'What for? If we want to read about it we can read out of this book here. We don't have to write it all out.'

'I asked you not to call out, and if you have time you can draw a picture of one of these urns here, on page eighteen, or these coins at the bottom of the page . . . .'

'It's a waste of time.'

'Now look I've had enough of this calling out, you're

the one who's wasting time. Get started or you'll still be here when the bell goes.'

'Not me, I start work at four . . . .'

'Not me either I'm going home to get ready . . . .'

'And that boy there, Pele, get that hat off.'

'He can't Miss he's sister gave him a kina.'

'Now you heard me, get it off, you're supposed to be in uniform. That's not part of your uniform . . . .'

'But Miss we all haven't . . . .'

'None of us is in uniform.'

'See Juliet with her jandals on and Va with a tee shirt and Junior with a green jersey . . . .'

'Besides it's very bad manners, now get it off.'

'Who said it's bad manners?'

'Hey Pele boy you got bad manners.'

'No I hafn't, I got a kina.'

'Hey Pele you forgot to say ''Peel-eeze''.'

'You forgot to say ''Tha-ank you''.'

'Now stop all this nonsense. None of you have got any manners whatsoever, and I'm waiting for you Pele, to get that hat off.'

'He can't Miss it's stuck on his head.'

'He's whole head'll come off Miss.'

'Hey Miss it's nearly bell time.'

'Come here Pele. I'm going to see Mr Sutton about you in a minute.'

'What for Miss?'

'For being rude and ill-mannered, now give me that hat.'

'I hafn't got it Miss.'

Because he has taken it off and passed it behind him to Juliet who passed it back to George. George toed it across to Francie who stared at the wall and passed it to Nga who passed it to Va.

'Well where is it, what did you do with it?'

'I don't know Miss, it's gone.'

'Don't you lie to me, you've given it to someone. Where is it Juliet?'

'I don't know Miss.'

'Now someone in this room has got it and whoever it is had better own up very quickly.'

And Va passed it to Peter who passed it to Junior who sits by the door.

'Well, I've had enough of this class and its rudeness and nonsense, and no one is leaving this room until I get that hat . . . .'

'Except me, I'm going to work at four . . . .'

'Except no one, now you can all just sit there and . . . .'

'And I'm catching the bus . . . .'

'All right I'll wait, and you'll all wait. No one leaves this room until I find out who's got the hat . . . .'

People of Ancient Greece had ideas and coins and urns and acting and poetry, and messages on walls. Wall messages told truths, and you could look there if you wanted to know what was in your mind and heart. A door was slamming to and fro, and in the corridor Neville was trundling Valerie along to get her down the steps before three o'clock. Junior opened the door and tossed the hat.

'What are you doing, who said you could open the door? No one's to move until I get the hat, and I'm going to see Mr Sutton about this class . . . .'

'Hey Miss the bell's gone . . . .'

'No one's to move and no one's leaving this room . . . .'

'Except me . . . .'

'And me . . . .'

'I go to work at four . . . .'

'I catch the bus . . . .'

'I watch telly and I peel potatoes . . . .'
'I go to Peter's for a smoke . . . .'
'We go to "Friendship" . . . .'
'We go on a truck to collect rags and paper . . . .'
'There's going to be trouble over this, you'll all be in trouble, the whole class . . . .'

And I run to catch up to Neville and Valerie, running down the steps, jumping three at the bottom, fast past the parked cars and down the drive. Valerie has long white hair but her neck's on one side and her legs are no good.
'Vala-rie, Vala-rie, I want the hat back.'
'You look neat Pele, with your haircut.'
'Give us it Valerie.'
'But you look neat Pele, ay Neville.'
'He looks like a kina.'
'Give me it Valerie.'
'Take it then, get it off my head.'
'Hey Valerie, hey Neville and Dean, you want a smoke?'
'Have you got matches?'
'Junior's got matches.'
'You wait for Junior, then catch us up.'
'Hey dog, hey dog, come here and wait by me.'

Between Earth and Sky

I walked out of the house this morning and stretched my arms out wide. Look, I said to myself. Because I was alone except for you. I don't think you heard me.

Look at the sky, I said.

Look at the green earth.

How could it be that I felt so good? So free? So full of the sort of day it was? How?

And at that moment, when I stepped from my house, there was no sound. No sound at all. No bird call, or tractor grind. No fire crackle or twig snap. As though the moment had been held quiet, for me only, as I stepped out into the morning. Why the good feeling, with a lightness in me causing my arms to stretch out and out? How blue, how green, I said into the quiet of the moment. But why, with the sharp nick of bone deep in my back and the band of flesh tightening across my belly?

All alone. Julie and Tamati behind me in the house, asleep, and the others over at the swamp catching eels. Riki two paddocks away cutting up a tree he'd felled last autumn.

I started over the paddocks towards him then, slowly, on these heavy knotted legs. Hugely across the paddocks I went almost singing. Not singing because of needing every breath, but with the feeling of singing. Why, with the deep twist and pull far down in my back and cramping between the legs? Why the feeling of singing?

How strong and well he looked. How alive and strong, stooping over the trunk steadying the saw. I'd hated him for days, and now suddenly I loved him again but didn't know why. The saw cracked through the tree setting little splinters of warm wood hopping. Balls of mauve smoke lifted into the air. When he looked up I put my hands to my back and saw him understand me over the skirl of the saw. He switched off, the sound fluttered away.

I'll get them, he said.

We could see them from there, leaning into the swamp, feeling for eel holes. Three long whistles and they looked up and started towards us, wondering why, walking reluctantly.

Mummy's going, he said.

We nearly got one, Turei said. Ay Jimmy, ay Patsy, ay Reuben?

Yes, they said.

Where? said Danny.

I began to tell him again, but he skipped away after the others. It was good to watch them running and shouting through the grass. Yesterday their activity and noise had angered me, but today I was happy to see them leaping and shouting through the long grass with the swamp mud drying and caking on their legs and arms.

Let Dad get it out, Reuben turned, was calling. He can get the lambs out. Bang! Ay Mum, ay?

Julie and Tamati had woken. They were coming to meet us, dragging a rug.

Not you again, they said taking my bag from his hand.

Not you two again, I said. Rawhiti and Jones.

Don't you have it at two o'clock.

We go off at two.

Your boyfriends can wait.

Our sleep can't.

I put my cheek to his and felt his arm about my shoulders.

Look after my wife, he was grinning at them.

Course, what else.

Go on. Get home and milk your cows, next time you see her she'll be in two pieces.

I kissed all the faces poking from the car windows then stood back on the step waving. Waving till they'd gone. Then turning felt the rush of water.

Quick, I said. The water.

Water my foot; that's piddle.

What you want to piddle in our neat corridor for? Sit down. Have a ride.

Helped into a wheelchair and away, careering over the brown lino.

Stop. I'll be good. Stop I'll tell Sister.

Sister's busy.

No wonder you two are getting smart. Stop . . . .

That's it missus, you'll be back in your bikini by summer. Dr McIndoe.

And we'll go water-skiing together. Me.

Right you are. Well, see you both in the morning.

The doors bump and swing.

Sister follows.

Finish off girls. Maitland'll be over soon.

All right Sister.

Yes Sister. Reverently.

The doors bump and swing.

You are at the end of the table, wet and grey. Blood stains your pulsing head. Your arms flail in these new dimensions and your mouth is a circle that opens and closes as you scream for air. All head and shoulders and wide mouth screaming. They have clamped the few inches of cord which is all that is left of your old life now. They draw mucous and bathe your head.

Leave it alone and give it here, I say.

What for? Haven't you got enough kids already?

Course. Doesn't mean you can boss that one around.

We should let you clean your own kid up?

Think she'd be pleased after that neat ride we gave her. Look at the little hoha. God he can scream.

They wrap you in linen and put you here with me.

Well anyway, here you are. He's all fixed, you're all done. We'll blow. And we'll get them to bring you a cuppa. Be good.

The doors swing open.

She's ready for a cuppa Freeman.

The doors bump shut.

Now. You and I. I'll tell you. I went out this morning. Look, I said, but didn't know why. Why the good feeling. Why, with the nick and press of bone deep inside. But now I know. Now I'll tell you and I don't think you'll mind. It wasn't the thought of knowing you, and having you here close to me that gave me this glad feeling, that made me look upwards and all about as I stepped out this morning. The gladness was because at last I was to be free. Free from that great hump that was you, free from the aching limbs and swelling that was you. That was why this morning each stretching of flesh made me glad.

And freedom from the envy I'd felt, watching him these past days, stepping over the paddocks whole and strong. Unable to match his step. Envying his bright striding. But I could love him again this morning.

These were the reasons each gnarling of flesh made me glad as I came out into that cradled moment. Look at the sky, look at the earth, I said. See how blue, how green. But I gave no thought to you.

And now. You sleep. How quickly you have learned this quiet and rhythmic breathing. Soon they'll come and put a cup in my hand and take you away.

You sleep, and I too am tired, after our work. We worked hard you and I and now we'll sleep. Be close. We'll sleep a little while ay, you and I.

Mirrors

So out under a hanging sky with my neck in danger from the holes in my slippers. Hey slippers. Watch out now, we've both seen younger days remember. Hurry me down to the end of the drive for the milk. Milk. Then turn me and we'll scuff back inside together to where the heater's plugged, pressing a patch of warmth into the corner where I'll sit with my back to the window, drinking tea. By gee.

Woke early this morning into shouldered silence with light just signing in, and thought how it was, how it could be, to sit silent in a silent house, in a warm corner drinking tea. Just me.

Or instead, I thought, I could as usual sleep. And wake in an hour to the foot thuds and voice noise. Doors and drawers, and perhaps with his arm reaching to turn me towards him. But my feet made up my mind. Poking from under the covers ready to find the floor, dangling. Two limp fillets of cod. How did you get like that feet? That shape, that colour — haven't seen you since the summer and don't know you lately. We found the floor and poked you into these two grinners, or gaspers. Shuffled to the wardrobe for a gown and then to the bathroom to wash.

Six drops no more, and only to keep the record straight. Because I nag them in the mornings. In the mornings I issue lists — to flush the toilet, to wash, to comb. Not to swing on chairs, to grab, eat like pigs, fight. But none of that this early morning. No lists, no

nagging. This next half hour's mine. Only six I promise, a quick flick is all.

Into the kitchen. Plug the heater, plug the jug. What
shall it be, coffee or tea? What do you say slippers? —
your tongues hang out like mine.

Yes tea, but you see, no milk.

Can't spoil the cup for want of. Milk. And it'll only
take a moment, unplug the jug. Step quietly, sleep has
ears remember. Trip me and it'll be the end of you two
I promise, trippers. Turn handle and out. Out under a
sky filled and sagging.

Dog next door is up before me and in a bad mood this
morning. Anyway I don't want to talk to him, I'm hurrying. He turns his back and huffs, snuffing the ground,
big footing through silvered grass and scaring a bird.
That was perhaps finding a snail to take and knock on
stone. Leaving little specked brown shell pieces splintered on rock, and the morsel gone.

And cat prints ahead of me too. Cautious stars in the
soft soil where the garden begins — she's dug a hole
there perhaps, somewhere among the rusting silver beet
and the holed cabbages. Somewhere in the early hours
she excreted precisely, covered, and walked away.
Perhaps. After roaming the darkness, pressing out soft
stars on to the whole length and breadth of the night,
that's right. Eyes specked like cut onion.

Quickly now. And remember I've come only for
want of a few drops. Of milk. So I'll keep my mind on
it. The corner waits warm and quiet. A nudge of a
switch will set the jug uttering. So go. No time for star
gazing. Get flapping, flappers, it'll rain. See how the
sky reaches down. See its uncertainty — there a rinsing-
water colour that's not the telly ad kind with *diamanté*
bubbles rising and good enough to drink, but which is
the real kind, yes. From the tub full of jeans, or load of

jerseys and socks — and there, shot through with green, brown, black and purple. Growing and shrinking. Pocked and pimpled like mould. And I will sit warm listening to it, alone, the rain plunging, if I hurry. In a warm corner with my throat scalded by the flowing of hot liquid.

Here now, and I can reach into the box. For milk. Turn my back and go. No need this morning to look past the gate, over the road to the sea, to see, to determine its mood, find out about the island. They'll both be there mid-morning, tomorrow, next year, so go. But no, the gulls rise screaming.

See how they beat their wings into the wind this morning, their legs dangles useless like shreds of red or yellow balloon before they tuck them out of sight.

And now my eyes are spiked, winkled out from their sockets on bright pins, and swivelling. See how the horizon is buckled by the waves' leaping, and how the waves ride in bumper to bumper each side of the island, then forget which way to go. Face each other snarling. Pounce and fall back, chop and slap.

Kung Fu Fighting,
Yes, Yes,
Kung Fu Fighting,
Yes, Yes.

The island like the old dog grouching, in a bad mood this morning.

But nearer to shore the waves remember and re-assemble, find the right curve and come gnashing in like great grinning mouthfuls of teeth. Heaping wads of weed on to the shore and tossing out white sticks. And further along they climb stacked rocks and splinter into marbled drops, wind hanging, then slow motion falling. Fingering in over ledges and into crevices, then evacuating as small stones roll and spin.

And this afternoon the children will walk there, take up the white sticks and stir the weed heaps to spark the small firework displays of leaping sand fleas.

They'll turn the tessellating stones for sticky fish which will play dead even after being pressed quite firmly with prising thumbs. They'll look into the rioting water for new things because once there was a netted glass ball from Japan, and once a bag of drowned cats, and once a corked bottle which could have contained a message but didn't. Once there was a condom floating, rim upward, which didn't look so out of place really and could have been a herring or a cod, open mouthed, coming to the surface to feed.

And they'll yell out over the water I wish it was summer.

I want to come in.

Wish it was summer.

I wish.

Summer.

I want I want.

I wish.

And they'll see their words curl in under the waves' furl and watch the words hurled back fragmented at their feet retreating.

And now there is the first drop, on the back of my hand as I turn. Hurry now. Safely do you hear. Next door's plum has one white flower and twig ends groaning. She'll be home tomorrow with her new baby and a bagful of black knitting.

I'm going, she'd yelled. But I came back for my knitting. And she had waved a plastic bag of needles and black skeins. So this minute while others sit in bed making white shells and fans, and loop up row upon row of holes in two-ply on twelves, she turns out an enormous black jersey cabled and twisted, for her husband who will be ashamed to have anything so wonderful. He will give it away and she will be pleased about the story she has to tell. There will be two flowers tomorrow perhaps, or more.

The next drop now, and there look. Damn dog. Hurry. I'm going to hit him hard with a bottle of milk. He sets himself at the top of the path, by the front door. He closes his eyes, hunches his shoulders and lowers his hind quarters as the stool elongates from under his tail. Hangs, as I come yelling, my neck in jeopardy. Slowly drops, coiling back on itself like a suicidal scorpion. He doesn't look at me, doesn't hear, but lowers his tail, lifts his head and walks off. His morosity parcelled away.

And all I wanted was a half hour I tell you, not great rain bullets fired at me as I look for a spade, not skin lumping from the cold and a mess to clean. Only a warm few moments and breathing in and out, drinking tea. Time to look at the folds in the curtains and to watch the grey reels of darkness rotating in the room's corners and growing paler. A time to be you see.

But now they'll be up. Opening and closing. Peeing, washing. Dressing. And he'll be on the march, opening windows. Letting fresh air in, instead of warm in bed. And I could have, if I'd thought, stayed. I'd have been warm right now and still asleep perhaps. Could have turned to him and we'd have coupled quite lazily. Warmly. Shared a quiet half hour, if.

But instead I make a vee-shaped hole with two thrusts of the spade while the rain assaults and the flesh bulges. Damn dog. Sat and shat. Then walked away, quite simply that.

Now look you've trodden in it, you'll feed the fire true you two. You're done for. I shunt what's left of dog into the vee and cover. I whip you two off and run

with you under the dispatching sky and throw you into
the incinerator. Goodbye. Then hose the wretched feet
blueing under the sudden slam of water.

And now I step in on to the mat, gasping, and they
have come to look at me.

Why?

Did you run round in the rain?

Barefooted?

In a dressing gown?

In pyjamas?

And leave the heater on?

And a cup. Waiting?

I'm in a mood, like dog — and island — and won't
answer.

They stare, then the boys go back to their hunt for
football jerseys. Two diving in the washing and the
other hanging from a shelf in the hot-water cupboard.
And I won't help them, won't say folded on the top
shelf. Up there. The two little ones will not take their
eyes away from my mood. They stare.

So at last I tell them grumpily I trod in it and had to
hose my feet. And throw my slippers in the incinerator.
Dog bog.

Dog bog? Their faces flower.

What colour was it?

We found a white one once.

On the footpath outside the shop.

We took half each.

To draw with.

On the road.

But it broke.

And fell into crumbs.

They want me to laugh but I'm flinging off clothes
and rubbing my hair. Why should I laugh? Why don't

they leave me alone? Pickers. Naggers.

And the other two will get up soon and yell about the noise that's going on. They'll turn on their music and grumble.

In the kitchen and lounge the back windows are open and fresh air pours in. He is striding, but stops to look at me, and at the mood I'm in.

Your feet, he says. Put something on them. Slippers.

She burnt them.

She trod in dog shit and now her slippers are in the incinerator.

For burning.

Burning.

He is all washed and combed and vigorous looking; the jug steams and he has made the porridge. His eyes are full of what he will do this morning zipped into an oilskin and booted to the knees. Mirrored I see two barrow loads of seaweed for the garden, forked out, spread and reeking. A trench for the kitchen scraps and two new rows of cabbage plants.

Now the three boys are in, geared for their games.

Burning?

Your slippers?

Why?

Waiting for me to break silence, to cry perhaps, or laugh.

He has gone out and returned with a pair of his socks, his fingertips touching over the ball that the socks have been rolled into.

Put them on. We'll feed these ones and have a cup of tea before the other two get up. Grumbling. Turning their songs up loud.

And along with the seaweed and the scrap trench and

the planted cabbages, I see mirrored I missed you this morning. And could have had a half hour quiet, together.

We play at ten.

The three of us. At ten.

If the rain stops.

And this afternoon I'm going down the beach.

To see.

To find something from Japan.

I wish I saw.

The dog.

Bog.

So I pull the socks over the two fillets of feet, purpled, and shut two windows.

On the plum tree. Next door, I say. There's one new flower. And twig ends all ready to heave.

Beans

Every Saturday morning in the winter term I bike into
town to play Rugby. Winter's a great time. We live
three miles out of town and the way in is mostly
uphill, so I need to get a good early start to be in town
by nine. On the way in I don't get a chance to look
around me or notice things very much because the
going is fairly hard. Now and again where it gets a bit
steep I have to stand up on the pedals and really tread
hard.

But it's great getting off to Rugby on a Saturday
morning with my towel and change on the carrier, and
pushing hard to get there by nine. It's great.

By the time I get to the grounds I'm really puffing
and I know my face is about the colour of the club-
house roof. But I'm ready to go on though. I can't
wait to get on the field and get stuck into the game; I
really go for it. I watch that ball and chase it all over
the place. Where the ball goes I go. I tackle, handle,
kick, run, everything. I do everything I can think of
and I feel good. Sometimes it's cold and muddy and
when I get thrown down into the mud and come up all
mucky I feel great, because all the mud shows that I've
really made a game of it. The dirtier I get the better I
like it because I don't want to miss out on anything.

Then after the game I strip off and get under the
shower in the club-room, and sometimes the water is
boiling hot and sometimes cold as anything. And
whatever it is, you're hopping up and down and get-

ting clean, and yelling out to your mates about the game and saying is it hot or cold in your one.

I need a drink then. I get a drink from the dairy across the road and the dairy's always jammed full of us boys getting drinks. You should hear the noise, you should really hear it.

The going home is one of the best parts of all. I hop on my bike and away I go, hardly any pushing at all. Gee it's good. I can look about me and see everything growing. Cabbages and caulis, potatoes and all sorts of vegetables. And some of the paddocks are all ploughed up and have rows of green just showing through. All neat and tidy, and not much different to look at from the coloured squares of knitting my sister does for girl guides. You see all sorts of people out in the gardens working on big machines or walking along the rows weeding and hoeing: that's the sort of place it is around here. Everything grows and big trucks take all the stuff away, then it starts all over again.

But, I must tell you. Past all the gardens about a mile and a half from where I live there's a fairly steep rise. It's about the steepest part on the way home and I really have to puff up that bit. Then I get to the top and there's a long steep slope going down. It's so steep and straight it makes you want to yell and I usually do. That's not all though. Just as you start picking up speed on the down slope you get this great whiff of pigs. Poo. Pigs. It makes you want to laugh and shout it's such a stink. And as I go whizzing down the stretch on my bike I do a big sniff up, a great big sniff, and get a full load of the smell of pigs. It's such a horrible great stink that I don't know how to describe it. We've got a book in our library at school and in it there's a poem about bells and the poem says 'joyous'. 'The joyous ringing of bells' or 'bells ringing joyously', something like that. Well 'joyous' is the word I think of when I smell the pigs. Joyous. A joyous big stink of pigs. It's really great.

It's not far to my place after I've taken the straight. When I get home I lean my bike up against the shed and I feel really hot and done for. I don't go straight inside though. Instead I flop myself down on the grass underneath the lemon tree and I pick a lemon and take a huge bite of it. The lemons on our tree are as sour as sour, but I take a big bite because I feel so good. It makes me pull awful faces and roll over and over in the grass, but I keep on taking big bites until the lemon is all gone, skin and everything. Then I pick another lemon and eat that all up too because I don't want to miss a thing in all my life.

We have an old lady living next to us. She's pretty old and she doesn't do much except walk around her garden. One day I heard her say to Mum, 'He's full of beans that boy of yours. Full of beans.'

Letters from Whetu

Dear Lenny,

> Be like Whetu o te Moana,
> Beat Boredom,
> Write a Letter.

How slack finding myself the only one of the old gang in the sixth form. How slack and BORING. And it's so competitive round here — No chance of copying a bit of homework or sharing a few ideas. Everyone's after marks and grades coz that's what counts on ACCREDITING DAY and Nobody Never tells Nobody Nothing — No Way. ACCREDITING DAY — it's ages away yet everyone's in a panic. It's like we're all going to be sorted out for heaven or hell, or for DECIDING DAY, and I really don't know what it's all for. I've thought and thought but just don't get it. I tell yuh it just doesn't add up. Must tell you about DECIDING DAY inaminnit.

See ... it seems we get put through this machine so that we can come out well-educated and so we can get interesting jobs. I think it's supposed to make us better than some other people — like our mothers and fathers for example, and some of our friends. And somehow

it's supposed to make us happier and more FULFILL-
ED. Well I dunno.

I quite like Fisher, I kind of appreciate her even
though she thinks she, and she alone, got me through
S.C. last year, and even though she thinks I've got no
brayne of my own. Little does she know that I often
wish now that I'd fayled. How was I to know I'd be
sitting here alone and so lonely learning boring things.
Why do we learn such boring things? We learned boring
things last year and now we're learning boring things
again. I bet this letter's getting boring.

I sometimes do a bit of a stir with Fisher, like I say
'yous' instead of 'you' (pl.). It always sends her PUR-
PLE. The other day I wrote it in my essay and she had a
BLUE fit. She scratched it out in RED and wrote me a
double underlined note — 'I have told you many times
before that there is no such word as "yous" (I wonder
if it hurt her to write it). Please do not use (yous heh
heh) it again.' So I wrote a triple underlined note
underneath — 'How can I yous it if it does not exist?'
Now that I think of it that's really slack — what lengths
I go to, it's really pathetic. I mean she's OKAY, but
I'm a bit sick of being her honourable statistic, her
minority person MAKING IT.

I'll tell you something else, that lady sure does go on.
And on. And on. She's trying to make us enjoy K.M.
Kay Em is what she calls Katherine Mansfield, as
though she and K.M. were best mates. Well I suppose
Fisher could be just about old enough to have been a
mate of K.M.s . . . . I'll tell you what she's doing. She's
prancing about reading like she's gonna bust. Her lips
are wobbling and popping, and she's sort of poised like
an old ballet dancer. She does a couple of tip-toes now
and again. Sometimes she flaps the book about and

makes circles in the air with it. I don't think she'll burst into tears.

Do you know what? When she waves and flaps the book about she doesn't stop 'reading', so I suppose that means she knows her K.M. off by heart, bless her HART (Halt All Racist Tours), punctuation and all. I don't think her glasses will quite fall off — Beat Boredom, wait and hope for Fisher's glasses to fall off and cut her feet to ribbons.

Gee I enjoyed our day at the beach last weekend, and us being all together again first time for ages. Andy looks great. All those hours in the sea and those big waves lopping over us. Hey why don't we save up and get us a surfboard?

I got my beans when I got home though, boy did I get my beans. Yes, and we'll take some food next time, and some togs and towels (to save our jeans from getting so clean). What about this weekend, but we'd have to contact Andy. Anyhows think on it. Really neat. It wuz tanfastic bowling round in those breakers hour after hour.

And what about those new songs we made up — haven't done that since fourth form. Soon as I got home, after having my ears laid back by Mum and Dad, I went and wrote that second song down so we wouldn't forget it. I like it, I really do. I'm writing out a copy for each of us and I'm sending Andy's with his letter which I'll write period 4. I'm writing letters to all of you today. Gonna post them too, even though I see you all at lunchtime (except Andy).

Can't remember the words to that first song, there must've been about twenty verses, and what rubbish. I can remember the 'Shake-a Shake-a' and the 'Culley bubba' bits, and I remember Iosefa's verse,

Tasi lua tolu fa,
Come a me a hugga hugga,
Shake-a Shake-a Shake-a,
Culley bubba longa-a long-a.

And

Tangaroa Tangaroa,
Little fish belong-a he a,
Shake-a Shake-a . . . .

Then there was another one about a shitting seagull — well never mind. Great music you and Andy made for it though, and only the waves to hear.

She's still flapping, and poncing, and I swear there's a tear in her eye.

And yes. I said I was going to tell you about DECID-ING DAY. Went to the library on Monday, and opened a book which I started reading in the middle some-where. Well this story is all set in New Zealand in the future ay, and there's been a world war and wide devas-tation.

There are too many people and they're short of stuff — goods, manure, natural resources and all that, so it's been agreed that all the cripples, mentals, wrinklies and sickies have to be sorted out and killed, then recy-cled. DECIDING DAY is the day the computer comes up with who's human and who's 'animal'. They're going to make them (the dead mentals, etc.) into energy, and use their skins for purses, etc. The kid down the road becomes your new knife handles, buy a bottle of drink and it's your granny stoppered inside ready to fizz. Turn on your light and there's your nutty uncle. After that there'll be a perfect society and a life of ease so they reckon. Neat story?

After DECIDING DAY the fires are going for weeks and weeks, and there's smoke and stink everywhere. The remaining people (not very many coz the computer doesn't find too many 'humans') try to make out they can handle it, but they can't. They can't hack it at all, and they want to chunder over and over, or fall about mad screaming.

Well e hoa. Fisher's winding down, and period one almost over. Love talking to you, not bored at all. See you lunchtime but you won't get this til next week. Gonna get me some envelopes and stamps and do some lickin'.

Arohanui,
Whetu o te Moana.
(I was named after a church.)

Mathematics,
Room 68,
Period 2.
Friday.

Dear Ani,

The new maths teacher is really strange. He never calls the roll but just barges in, goes straight to the rolling blackboard and starts writing. At the same time as he's writing he's mumbling into his whiskers and flinging the board up. His face is only about six inches from the board and you keep thinking he might catch his nose in it. I think he's half blind.

When he gets to the end of the rolling board he starts rubbing out with his left hand and keeps on scribbling his columns and numbers with his right. At the same time he keeps up his muttering and his peering. All he needs now is a foot drum and some side cymbals. When the bell goes he turns round as if he's just noticed us, his specs are all white and chalky and his whiskers are snowy, and he has a tiny pyramid of chalk pinched between his finger and thumb, all that's left of a whole stick. What a weird-o. Then he yells out page numbers and exercise numbers for homework and says, 'Out you go. Quickly.' As we go out he's cleaning his bi-fokes and getting out a new piece of chalk ready for the next lot of suckers. No wonder I'm no good at maths (not like Lenny who's got a mthmtcl brayne. What say we save up for a srfbrd and Lenny can be the treasurer).

Trust you to get stuck halfway up the cliff. Hey I got really scared looking at you, then I got wild with the boys just leaving you there and doing all that Juliet stuff with the guitar. Wasn't til I started up to help you that they decided to come up, and even so they were only assing round.

Then it was really beautiful up on that ledge after all. Wasn't it? You forget, living here. Living here you never really see the sun go down, or you don't think of it as being anything really good. Sometimes if you're outside picking up the newspaper or the milk bottles you see the sky looking a bit pink, or else it just gets dark and you know it's happened. But you don't think 'The sun's going down,' you only think 'It's getting dark.' Mostly we have the curtains over the windows because of people going past, and you think they might LOOK IN, or something TERRIBLE like that. And what if one of them HAD A GUN, and aimed it at you? What if there was a loud bang, and a little hole in the window the size of a peanut, and a big one in your head the size of an orange? What a splash of colour, what a sunset and a half that would be.

Yes and anyway we need the curtains over the windows because of telly being on. Telly is a sort of window too, with everything always on the other side of the glass. After a while you don't know the difference between 'looking out' and 'looking in'. Well you know what I mean fren, you don't ever think how it is sitting halfway up a cliff making up songs, with the sun dropping behind an island.

You weren't scared anymore once we all got up there, and the sun settled at the head of the island like a big bloodshot eye just for a sec. Then it dropped behind like a trick ball.

You don't ever think of the sky slapped all over red and orange, and the sea smothered in gold-pink curls. When you think back you can see it all again, but can't quite feel the same, like your skin is stretching tight over your body, like your eyes are just holes and it's all pouring in.

Well what a climb down in the dark, then the hunt in the dark for shoes. If we hadn't had to look for our shoes we'd have caught an earlier train home. God I got my beans when I got home. Then of course there was that long wait in the greasy shop for our greasies. I was *starving*.

When we were little we always used to go to the beach — every low tide even in the cold weather. But now that us kids have grown up I don't think Dad likes it anymore. Anyway he's so busy and on so many committees — marae committee, P.T.A., Tu Tangata, District Council — and Mum's almost as bad. We're never home together these days, especially now that Hepa's flatting and Amiria's married. As for Koro, he's never in one place for a day. He gets called north south east west, if not to a tangi then to a land meeting, if not to a land meeting then to a convention. Well it's no wonder we never get to the beach or see each other much.

Er um! Hepa turned up on Saturday, so Dad went and got Amiria and John. Er! Koro was back from Auckland, so, er, I was the only one not home. And NOBODY knew where I was. Tricky huh? Well we didn't know we were going to the beach did we? We started out to meet beautiful Andy off the train and ended up getting the next train north.

Hey old chalk-chewer is yelling out page numbers, he's remembered we're here. He looks like a sort of constipated old Santa—I'd better end this letter inaminnit.

Yes Dad cracked a fit and I took a good bit of flak from Mum as well. They were all dressed to go out and they'd been waiting hours for me. Of course what Dad really thought was that I was out getting myself popped, it's what they all think but won't say. Ding Dong. Got to bed midnight. Or was that the time we got home, heh heh?

The beach. It beats late shopping nights by a long way. Gotta go. I'm the only one left, goodbye fren. Writing to Iosefa next period. See you lunchtime, but you won't get this til next week.

Much love,
Yours ake, ake, ake,
Star.

(I'm a Star
I'm a Star
I'm a Mon*star*.)

Geography,
Room 3,
Period 3.
Friday.

Dear Sef,

I write to you amid a shower of topographical
maps, aerial photos, fault lines and air masses. What a
circus. Lattimer arrives loaded with books which he
bangs on to a table. Then he starts spouting — So you
SEE, So you SEE — producing his cross-sections,
graphs, map keys, land formations like tricks out of a
hat. After a while he bounces round the room dealing
out worksheets and slamming books down in front of
us, creating his own earthquakes.

Writing to Ani I remembered how we always used to
go downtown on late shopping nights. She and I used to
make up all sorts of excuses so we'd be allowed to go,
and so did you. You used to tell your mother you were
going on a training run, then you'd run into town and
we'd all meet and spend our money on take-aways and
junk. Then we'd hang round the fountain with the other
kids and hope a fight might start up between our college
and the one up the line. We always knew who was out
to get who, and who was ripping off what from where.
The night we caught the taxi home (with Lenny's
money) you had to run up and down the road to get
puffed and sweaty before you went inside. I got home
wet from you throwing half the fountain on me. We'd
all swapped clothes as usual.

Well parents get upset about funny things. Wasn't
allowed downtown for ages and ages and used to feel
really slacked off on late-shopping-nite-nites because I
wanted to be out there having FUN, that was winter.
Hey what babies we were, running round, hiding in

doorways and hoping all the time that something really awful would happen.

Yes Lattimer's got a great act there. Maybe we should all crouch on our desks like circus tigers and spring from table to table and roar, and swipe the air with our paws.

What about the time we took your little cousins to the zoo, and Andy got smart to the ape and it went haywire. Then Andy walked away whistling and looking at the sky. Remember the ducks zooming in, and the tiger that turned its bum round at feed time and pissed on the people. And Ani pissed herself laughing. Oh Ani, what a roly-poly, what a ball. Ani's really neat.

Well the ape was bouncing all over its cage with its big open mouth as pink as undercoat paint, baring his old smoker's teeth and trying to wrench the bars apart. Then he began snatching and grabbing at his own arm, his own shoulder, his own head, and at the same time he kept opening his mouth and slamming it shut, and putting his bottom teeth almost up his nose. His eyes were as black as print and glinting like flicked pins.

Our mate Lenny looked at the ape and said, 'Honey baby come to my pipi farm and I'll give you a gink at my muscles.' Spare it! Poor monkey, with its thumbs on back to front. The palms of its hands looked like old cow turds.

I really wonder about Lattimer. The way he throws himself about the room you'd think he was really trying to knock the walls down and make a run for it, or perhaps he wants to give himself a crack on the head so he can be pulled out by the feet.

Anyway he's all right — busts out in a sick grin every so often. Remember Harris (harass) and her screwed-up face, and how she used to walk in and shove open all the windows because we all stank. I really wanted to walk out that time Andy left, if only I'd had the guts. Everytime she got on to him I felt like dying, even before I knew Andy properly. She'd never believe what Andy's really like, she was just so scared of him, of his looks, of the way he talks, of his poor clothes. Most of all she must have realised Andy had her taped, over and over, although he never said anything. On that last day I reckon it was his quietness and his acceptance that got to her. She was screwed up with hate, and screaming. Writing to Andy next period and won't forget to tell him about Palmer's DISGUISE.

Sometimes I can't hack the thought that I didn't follow Andy down the road that day, instead of sitting here waiting to 'realise' my 'potential'. Hey Sef, when and how does potential become whatever it's meant to become? I mean Mum and Dad have all these IDEAS, they're both getting their THRILLS over my education and I reckon I'll be sitting behind a desk FOREVER.

Funny though, if it had been either one of them they'd have gone out the door with Andy without thinking twice, because they really know what's important. It's only me they've got under glass. Anyhows I'll leave it before I start thinking what a sucker I am.

And now I'll talk about the beach. Nex' time we'll take all our gears, especially FOOD. If you're wrkng next wknd, or if Ani's wrkng, or if Andy can't come, we'll go another time. Soon. But gee Sef, the dropping sun and the bleeding sky and those great fat humping seas, the seagulls . . . .

I often dream about flying, and sometimes in the dream I'm afraid of what I'm doing, and other times I'm so happy and free flying about, up above everyone and everything, going anywhere I want . . . . If I wasn't me I'd be a seagull belting out over the sea and throwing myself at any storm, ANY STORM. What would you be, e hoa, if you weren't you?

Gotta go Iosefa, he's snapping up all his books and handouts, and now, slurp, they're all back in the trick box. Howzat? See ya lunchtime, which is now.

Much love from,
Star of the Sea.

History,
Room 42,
Period 4.
Friday.

Dear Andy,

Great to see you on Sunday, you and your old guitar. I hardly remember going to the beach, only being there. When we came to meet you off the train we didn't quite expect to find ourselves on the next one heading north. Suddenly we were off the train again and legging it to the beach all those miles. But it seemed no distance, the road just rolled away under us and only our talking tongues were in a sweat. Hey that neat car, 'You got the Mercedes, I got the Benz' (according to Len). I've been writing letters all morning as part of my anti-boredom campaign.

What I want to tell you is that Iosefa has got a black eye. On Tuesday, Palmer, who is the new VICE principal, disguised himself (as a flasher) and pounced on Lenny, Iosefa and some other boys who were all puffing up large on the bank by the top field. True. He put on an old raincoat, ankle length no less (a real flasher's job), and one of those work caps that have advertisements printed on them — Marple Paints. The boys thought it was a member of the public taking a short-cut to the road so didn't take much notice. Instead it was old P. ready to pounce, wearing his usual greaser's grin.

All the letters went home to parents as usual — 'Dear   , I wish to bring to your notice that your son/daughter   was discovered (!!!) smoking in the school grounds on   (date, etc., etc.).'

Iosefa got thumped by his old man, and Lenny's mum screwed up the letter and laughed her wrinkled old head off. On Wednesday Palmer's blackboard was covered with compliments — 'Palmer's a wanker' and all the usual things. Someone drew a spy glass with a gory eye looking through. And you know Rick Ossler? His old man came up and shook 'the letter' in Palmer's face and called him a Creeping Jesus. Well I laughed and laughed. Never heard that expression before, but when I told Mum she said it was an oldie.

Anyway enough of that. Neat fun sitting up on that ledge singing up large, we must've been there for hours. Every now and then I'd think of all our mates from fourth form days, and how we'd all go over to D6 and sing and act like fools, and make up funny songs.

But Angie and Brian, Willy, Judy, Vasa, Hariata, lots of others . . . I was thinking too of how we all used to terrorise the town on late-shopping-nite-nites. Wonder what they're all doing now?

Before I went to bed on Saturday (and after I'd had my ears blasted for being back late), I wrote down the words of our song so we wouldn't forget them. It seems there are things to know about our songs, even the rubbish ones, things we don't really know yet. There are so many things to know, and I really envy you because you're learning some of them. I want to know important things, and also I want to know what's important.

Slitting the throat of a sheep and hanging it up kicking seems to be a real thing, like picking watercress, and even though it's something you can do and I can't, I still want to know about it. Even though I wouldn't want to cut the belly and haul the guts out I know it must sometimes be all right to have blood on your hands. Or if not blood then dirt, or shit — on the outside where you can see it. You see I've got this bad idea that I'm sitting here storing all the muck up inside me, getting slowly but surely shit ridden. As for you, you've never held any shit, ever, and never will.

But other things, so many things. I mean, I want to know what goes on in houses, especially in houses on hills with trees round them. What do the people there say to each other? What do they laugh about and what do they eat? Are their heads different from them being up higher? Do they chew gum, how can I know?

Are girls who work in clothes shops just like me, or do their faces fall away when night comes, and does someone hang them limp on a rack until morning? Does central heating dry people out and make them unable to face the weather? Well I could go on and on.

E hoa, I want to walk all over the world but how do I develop the skills for it sitting in a plastic bag fastened with a wire-threaded paper twist to keep the contents airtight. You sit cramped in there, with your head bowed, knees jack-knifed up under your chin.

If I walked round the world I'd wear two holes in my face in place of eyes and let everything pour in. I reckon I could play an alpine horn.

The other day two fifth formers bought pot from the caretaker then potted him. And a lot of fourth formers are getting high from sniffing cleaner fluid which they pour on their sleeves. Peter got his arm blown up when his mate lit a cigarette, and now he's in hospital (luckily). Were we *that* suicidal two years ago, screaming round town in our jackets wishing to see someone slit from eye to knee with a knife?

I saw a girl nick a bottle of the stuff from a stand in McKenzies yesterday but I didn't do anything. There were two rows of it on a glass shelf at 89c a bottle.

And now the bell rings and we're almost through the day. No more letters to write, but next period (last one) I'll write out THE SONG for everyone (see yours below). If I write slow enough it might use up the hour.

Well dear friend, write back straight away and tell us when you can come down again. WE'VE GOT PLANS, and WE SEND OUR LOVE.

> Yours 4 eva,
> Whetu.

> Sky love earth
> Shine light
> Fall rai-ai-ain,
> Earth give life
> Turn breast
> To chi-i-ild.
>
> Child
> Steal light
> Turn away rai-ai-ain,
> Thrust bright
> Sword
> Deep into ea-ea-earth.
>
> Mother bleed
> Your child
> Die,
> Bleed mother
> Child
> Already dead.
> > W-o-te-M.

It Used to be Green Once

We were all ashamed of our mother. Our mother always did things to shame us. Like putting red darns in our clothes, and cutting up old swimming togs and making two — girl's togs from the top half for my sister, and boy's togs from the bottom half for my brother. Peti and Raana both cried when Mum made them take the togs to school. Peti sat down on the road by our gate and yelled out she wasn't going to school. She wasn't going swimming. I didn't blame my sister because the togs were thirty-eight chest and Peti was only ten.

But Mum knew how to get her up off the road. She yelled loudly, 'Get up off that road my girl. There's nothing wrong with those togs. I didn't have any togs when I was a kid and I had to swim in my nothings. Get up off your backside and get to school.' Mum's got a loud voice and she knew how to shame us. We all dragged Peti up off the road before our mates came along and heard Mum. We pushed Peti into the school bus so Mum wouldn't come yelling up the drive.

We never minded our holey fruit at first. Dad used to pick up the cases of over-ripe apples or pears from town that he got cheap. Mum would dig out the rotten bits, and then give them to us to take for play-lunch. We didn't notice much at first, not until Reweti from down the road yelled out to us one morning, 'Hey you fullas. Who shot your pears?' We didn't have anywhere to hide our lunch because we weren't allowed school bags until we got to high school. Mum said she wasn't buying fourteen school bags. When we went to high school we could have shoes too. The whole lot of us gave Reweti a good hiding after school.

However, this story is mainly about the car, and about Mum and how she shamed us all the time. The shame of rainbow darns and cut-up togs and holey fruit was nothing to what we suffered because of the car. Uncle Raz gave us the car because he couldn't fix it up any more, and he'd been fined because he lived in Auckland. He gave the car to Dad so we could drive our cream cans up to the road instead of pushing them up by wheelbarrow.

It didn't matter about the car not having brakes because the drive from our cowshed goes down in a dip then up to the gate. Put the car in its first gear, run it down from the shed, pick up a bit of speed, up the other side, turn it round by the cream stand so that it's pointing down the drive again, foot off the accelerator and slam on the handbrake. Dad pegged a board there to make sure it stopped. Then when we'd lifted the cans out on to the stand he'd back up a little and slide off down the drive — with all of us throwing ourselves in over the sides as if it were a dinghy that had just been pushed out into the sea.

The car had been red once because you could still see some patches of red paint here and there. And it used to have a top too, that you could put down or up. Our uncle told us that when he gave it to Dad. We were all proud about the car having had a top once. Some of the younger kids skited to their mates about our convertible and its top that went up and down. But that was before our mother started shaming us by driving the car to the shop.

We growled at Mum and we cried but it made no difference. 'You kids always howl when I tell you to get our shopping,' she said.

'We'll get it Mum. We won't cry.'

'We won't cry Mum. We'll carry the sack of potatoes.'

'And the flour.'

'And the bag of sugar.'

'And the rolled oats.'

'And the tin of treacle.'

'We'll do the shopping Mum.'

But Mum would say, 'Never mind, I'll do it myself.' And after that she wouldn't listen any more.

How we hated Wednesdays. We always tried to be sick on Wednesdays, or to miss the bus. But Mum would be up early yelling at us to get out of bed. If we didn't get up when we were told she'd drag us out and pull down our pyjama pants and set our bums on the cold lino. Mum was cruel to us.

Whoever was helping with the milking had to be back quickly from the shed for breakfast, and we'd all have to rush through our kai and get to school. Wednesday was Mum's day for shopping.

As soon as she had everything tidy she'd change into her good purple dress that she'd made from a Japanese bedspread, pull on her floppy brimmed blue sunhat and her slippers and galoshes, and go out and start up the car.

We tried everything to stop her shaming us all.

'You've got no licence Mum.'

'What do I want a licence for? I can drive can't I? I don't need the proof.'

'You got no warrant.'

'Warrant? What's warrant?'

'The traffic man'll get you Mum.'

'That rat. He won't come near me after what he did

to my niece. I'll hit him right over his smart head with a bag of riwais and I'll hit him somewhere else as well.' We never could win an argument with Mum.

Off she'd go on a Wednesday morning, and once out on the road she'd start tooting the horn. This didn't sound like a horn at all but more like a flock of ducks coming in for a feed. The reason for the horn was to let all her mates and relations along the way know she was coming. And as she passed each one's house, if they wanted anything they'd have to run out and call it out loud. Mum couldn't stop because of not having any brakes. 'E Kiri,' each would call. 'Mauria mai he riwai,' if they wanted spuds; 'Mauria mai he paraoa,' if they wanted bread. 'Mauria mai he tarau, penei te kaita,' hand spread to show the size of the pants they wanted Mum to get. She would call out to each one and wave to them to show she'd understood. And when she neared the store she'd switch the motor off, run into the kerbing and pull on the handbrake. I don't know how she remembered all the things she had to buy — I only know that by the time she'd finished, every space in that car was filled and it was a squeeze for her to get into the driver's seat. But she had everything there, all ready to throw out on the way back.

As soon as she'd left the store she'd begin hooting again, to let the whole district know she was on her way. Everybody would be out on the road to get their shopping thrown at them, or just to watch our mother go chuffing past. We always hid if we heard her coming.

The first time Mum's car and the school bus met was when they were both approaching a one-way bridge from opposite directions. We had to ask the driver to stop and give way to Mum because she had no brakes. We were all ashamed. But everyone soon got to know

Mum and her car and they always stopped whenever they saw her coming. And you know, Mum never ever had an accident in her car, except for once when she threw a side of mutton out to Uncle Peta and it knocked him over and broke his leg.

After a while we started walking home from school on Wednesdays to give Mum a good chance of getting home before us, and so we wouldn't be in the bus when it had to stop and let her past. The boys didn't like having to walk home but we girls didn't mind because Mr Hadley walked home too. He was a new teacher at our school and he stayed not far from where we lived. We girls thought he was really neat.

But one day, it had to happen. When I heard the honking and tooting behind me I wished that a hole would appear in the ground and that I would fall in it and disappear for ever. As Mum came near she started smiling and waving and yelling her head off. 'Anyone wants a ride,' she yelled, 'they'll have to run and jump in.'

We all turned our heads the other way and hoped Mr Hadley wouldn't notice the car with our mother in it, and her yelling and tooting, and the brim of her hat jumping up and down. But instead, Mr Hadley took off after the car and leapt in over the back seat on top of the shopping. Oh the shame.

But then one day something happened that changed everything. We arrived home to find Dad in his best clothes, walking round and grinning, and not doing anything like getting the cows in, or mending a gate, or digging a drain. We said, 'What are you laughing at Dad?' 'What are you dressed up for? Hey Mum what's the matter with Dad?'

'Your Dad's a rich man,' she said. 'Your Dad, he's just won fifty thousand dollars in a lottery.'

At first we couldn't believe it. We couldn't believe it. Then we all began running round and laughing and yelling and hugging Dad and Mum. 'We can have shoes and bags,' we said. 'New clothes and swimming togs, and proper apples and pears.' Then do you know what Dad said? Dad said, 'Mum can have a new car.' This really astounded and amazed us. We went numb with excitement for five minutes then began hooting and shouting again, and knocking Mum over.

'A new car!'

'A new car?'

'Get us a Packard Mum.'

'Or a De Soto. Yes, yes.'

Get this, get that . . . .

Well Mum bought a big shiny green Chevrolet, and Dad got a new cowshed with everything modernised and water gushing everywhere. We all got our new clothes — shoes, bags, togs — and we even started taking posh lunches to school. Sandwiches cut in triangles, bottles of cordial, crisp apples and pears, and yellow bananas.

And somehow all of us kids changed. We started acting like we were somebody instead of ordinary like before. We used to whine to Dad for money to spend and he'd always give it to us. Every week we'd nag Mum into taking us to the pictures, or if she was tired we'd go ourselves by taxi. We got flash bedspreads and a piano and we really thought we were neat.

As for the old car — we made Dad take it to the dump. We never wanted to see it again. We all cheered when he took it away, except for Mum. Mum stayed inside where she couldn't watch, but we all stood outside and cheered.

We all changed, as though we were really somebody, but there was one thing I noticed. Mum didn't change at all, and neither did Dad. Mum had a new car all right, and a couple of new dresses, and a new pair of galoshes to put over her slippers. And Dad had a new modern milking shed and a tractor, and some other gadgets for the farm. But Mum and Dad didn't change. They were the same as always.

Mum still went shopping every Wednesday. But instead of having to do all the shopping herself she was able to take all her friends and relations with her. She had to start out earlier so she'd have time to pick everyone up on the way. How angry we used to be when Mum went past with her same old sunhat and her heap of friends and relations, and them all waving and calling out to us.

Mum sometimes forgot that the new car had brakes, especially when she was approaching the old bridge and we were coming the opposite way in the school bus. She would start tooting and the bus would have to pull over and let her through. That's when all our aunties and uncles and friends would start waving and calling out. But some of them couldn't wave because they were too squashed by people and shopping, they'd just yell. How shaming.

There were always ropes everywhere over Mum's new car holding bags of things and shovel handles to the roof and sides. The boot was always hanging open because it was too full to close — things used to drop out on to the road all the time. And the new car — it used to be green once, because if you look closely you can still see some patches of green paint here and there.

Journey

He was an old man going on a journey. But not really so old, only they made him old buttoning up his coat for him and giving him money. Seventy-one that's all. Not a journey, not what you would really call a journey — he had to go in and see those people about his land. Again. But he liked the word Journey even though you didn't quite say it. It wasn't a word for saying only for saving up in your head, and that way you could enjoy it. Even an old man like him, but not what you would call properly old.

The coat was good and warm. It was second-hand from the jumble and it was good and warm. Could have ghosts in it but who cares, warm that's the main thing. If some old pakeha died in it that's too bad because he wasn't scared of the pakeha kehuas anyway. The pakeha kehuas they couldn't do anything, it was only like having a sheet over your head and going woo-oo at someone in the lavatory . . . .

He better go to the lavatory because he didn't trust town lavatories, people spewed there and wrote rude words. Last time he got something stuck on his shoe. Funny people those town people.

Taxi.

It's coming Uncle.

Taxi Uncle. They think he's deaf. And old. Putting more money in his pocket and wishing his coat needed buttoning, telling him it's windy and cold. Never mind, he was off. Off on his journey, he could get round town good on his own, good as gold.

Out early today old man.

Business young fulla.

Early bird catches the early worm.

It'll be a sorry worm young fulla, a sorry worm.

Like that is it?

Like that.

You could sit back and enjoy the old taxi smells of split upholstery and cigarette, and of something else that could have been the young fulla's hair oil or his b.o. It was good. Good. Same old taxi same old stinks. Same old shop over there, but he wouldn't be calling in today, no. And tomorrow they'd want to know why. No, today he was going on a journey, which was a good word. Today he was going further afield, and there was a word no one knew he had. A good wind today but he had a warm coat and didn't need anyone fussing.

Same old butcher and same old fruit shop, doing all right these days not like before. Same old Post Office where you went to get your pension money, but he always sent Minnie down to get his because he couldn't stand these old-age people. These old-age people got on his nerves. Yes, same old place, same old shops and roads, and everything cracking up a bit. Same old taxi. Same old young fulla.

How's the wife?

Still growling old man.

What about the kids?

Costing me money.

Send them out to work that's the story.

I think you're right you might have something there old man. Well here we are, early. Still another half hour to wait for the train.

Best to be early. Business.

Guess you're right.

What's the sting?

Ninety-five it is.

Pull out a fistful and give the young fulla full eyes. Get himself out on to the footpath and shove the door, give it a good hard slam. Pick me up later young fulla, ten past five. Might as well make a day of it, look round town and buy a few things.

Don't forget ten past five.

Right you are old man five ten.

People had been peeing in the subway the dirty dogs. In the old days all you needed to do to get on to the station was to step over the train tracks, there weren't any piss holes like this to go through, it wasn't safe. Coming up the steps on to the platform he could feel the quick huffs of his breathing and that annoyed him, he wanted to swipe at the huffs with his hand. Steam engines went out years ago.

Good sight though seeing the big engines come bellowing through the cutting and pull in squealing, everything was covered in soot for miles those days.

New man in the ticket office, looked as though he still had his pyjamas on under his outfit. Miserable looking fulla and not at all impressed by the ten-dollar note handed through to him. A man feels like a screwball yelling through that little hole in the glass and then trying to pick up the change that sourpuss has scattered all over the place. Feels like giving sourpuss the fingers, yes. Yes he knows all about those things, he's not deaf and blind yet, not by a long shot.

Ah warmth. A cold wait on the platform but the carriages had the heaters on, they were warm even though they stank. And he had the front half of the first carriage all to himself. Good idea getting away early. And right up front where you could see everything. Good idea coming on his own, he didn't want anyone fussing round looking after his ticket, seeing if he's warm and saying things twice. Doing his talking for him, made him sick. Made him sick them trying to walk slow so they could keep up with him. Yes he could see every-thing. Not many fishing boats gone out this morning and the sea's turning over rough and heavy — Tamatea that's why. That's something they don't know all these young people, not even those fishermen walking about on their decks over there. Tamatea a Ngana, Tamatea Aio, Tamatea Whakapau — when you get the winds — but who'd believe you these days. They'd rather stare at their weather on television and talk about a this and a that coming over because there's nothing else to believe in.

Now this strip here, it's not really land at all, it's where we used to get our pipis, any time or tide. But they pushed a hill down over it and shot the railway line across to make more room for cars. The train driver knows it's not really land and he is speeding up over this strip. So fast you wait for the nose dive over the edge into the sea, especially when you're up front like this looking. Well too bad. Not to worry, he's nearly old anyway and just about done his dash, so why to worry if they nose dive over the edge into the sea. Funny people putting their trains across the sea. Funny people making land and putting pictures and stories about it in the papers as though it's something spectacu-lar, it's a word you can use if you get it just right and he could surprise quite a few people if he wanted to. Yet other times they go on as though land is just a nothing. Trouble is he let them do his talking for him. If he'd gone in on his own last time and left those fusspots at home he'd have got somewhere. Wouldn't need to be going in there today to tell them all what's what.

Lost the sea now and coming into a cold crowd. This

is where you get swamped, but he didn't mind, it was
good to see them all get in out of the wind glad to be
warm. Some of his whanaungas lived here but he
couldn't see any of them today. Good job too, he didn't
want them hanging round wondering where he was off
to on his own. Nosing into his business. Some of the
old railway houses still there but apart from that everything new, houses, buildings, roads. You'd never know
now where the old roads had been, and they'd filled a
piece of the harbour up too to make more ground. A
short row of sooty houses that got new paint once in a
while, a railway shelter, and a lunatic asylum and that
was all. Only you didn't call it that these days, he'd
think of the right words in a minute.

There now the train was full and he had a couple of
kids sitting by him wearing plastic clothes, they were
gog-eyed stretching their necks to see. One of them had
a snotty nose and a wheeze.

On further it's the same — houses, houses — but
people have to have houses. Two or three
farms once, on the cold hills, and a rough road going
through. By car along the old road you'd always see a
pair of them at the end of the drive waving with their
hats jammed over their ears. Fat one and a skinny one.
Psychiatric hospital, those were the words to use these
days, yes don't sound so bad. People had to have
houses and the two or three farmers were dead now
probably. Maybe didn't live to see it all. Maybe died
rich.

The two kids stood swaying as they entered the first
tunnel, their eyes stood out watching for the tunnel's
mouth, waiting to pass out through the great mouth of
the tunnel. And probably the whole of life was like that,
sitting in the dark watching and waiting. Sometimes it
happened and you came out into the light, but mostly it

only happened in tunnels. Like now.

And between the tunnels they were slicing the hills away with big machines. Great-looking hills too and not an easy job cutting them away, it took pakeha determination to do that. Funny people these pakehas, had to chop up everything. Couldn't talk to a hill or a tree these people, couldn't give the trees or the hills a name and make them special and leave them. Couldn't go round, only through. Couldn't give life, only death. But people had to have houses, and ways of getting from one place to another. And anyway who was right up there helping the pakeha to get rid of things — the Maori of course, riding those big machines. Swooping round and back, up and down all over the place. Great tools the Maori man had for his carving these days, tools for his new whakairo, but there you are, a man had to eat. People had to have houses, had to eat, had to get from here to there — anyone knew that. He wished the two kids would stop crackling, their mothers dressed them in rubbish clothes that's why they had colds.

Then the rain'll come and the cuts will bleed for miles and the valleys will drown in blood, but the pakeha will find a way of mopping it all up no trouble. Could find a few bones amongst that lot too. That's what you get when you dig up the ground, bones.

Now the next tunnel, dark again. Had to make sure the windows were all shut up in the old days or you got a face full of soot.

And then coming out of the second tunnel that's when you really had to hold your breath, that's when you really had to hand it to the pakeha, because there was a sight. Buildings miles high, streets and steel and concrete and asphalt settled all round the great-looking curve that was the harbour. Water with ships on it, and roadways threading up and round the hills to layer on

layer of houses, even in the highest and steepest places.
He was filled with admiration. Filled with Admiration,
which was another word he enjoyed even though it
wasn't really a word for saying, but yes he was filled
right to the top — it made him tired taking it all in. The
kids too, they'd stopped crackling and were quite still,
their eyes full to exploding.

The snotty one reminded him of George, he had pop
eyes and he sat quiet not talking. The door would open
slowly and the eyes would come round and he would
say I ran away again Uncle. That's all. That's all for a
whole week or more until his mother came to get him
and take him back. Never spoke, never wanted anything. Today if he had time he would look out for
George.

Railway station much the same as ever, same old
platforms and not much cleaner than the soot days.
Same old stalls and looked like the same people in
them. Underground part is new. Same cafeteria, same
food most likely, and the spot where they found the
murdered man looked no different from any other spot.
Always crowded in the old days especially during the
hard times. People came there in the hard times to do
their starving. They didn't want to drop dead while they
were on their own most probably. Rather all starve
together.

Same old statue of Kupe with his woman and his
priest, and they've got the name of the canoe spelt
wrong his old eyes aren't as blind as all that. Same old
floor made of little coloured pieces and blocked into
patterns with metal strips, he used to like it but now he
can just walk on it. Big pillars round the doorway holding everything in place, no doubt about it you had to
hand it to the pakeha.

Their family hadn't starved, their old man had seen to

that. Their old man had put all the land down in garden, all of it, and in the weekends they took what they didn't use round by horse and cart. Sometimes got paid, sometimes swapped for something, mostly got nothing but why to worry. Yes great looking veges they had those days, turnips as big as pumpkins, cabbages you could hardly carry, big tomatoes, lettuces, potatoes, everything. Even now the ground gave you good things. They had to stay home from school for the planting and picking, usually for the weeding and hoeing as well. Never went to school much those days but why to worry.

Early, but he could take his time, knows his way round this place as good as gold. Yes he's walked all over these places that used to be under the sea and he's ridden all up and down them in trams too. This bit of sea has been land for a long time now. And he's been in all the pubs and been drunk in all of them, he might go to the pub later and spend some of his money. Or he could go to the continuous pictures but he didn't think they had them any more. Still, he might celebrate a little on his own later, he knew his way round this place without anyone interfering. Didn't need anyone doing his talking, and messing things up with all their letters and what not. Pigeons, he didn't like pigeons, they'd learned to behave like people, eat your feet off if you give them half a chance.

And up there past the cenotaph, that's where they'd bulldozed all the bones and put in the new motorway. Resited, he still remembered the newspaper word, all in together. Your leg bone, my arm bone, someone else's bunch of teeth and fingers, someone else's head, funny people. Glad he didn't have any of his whanaungas underground in that place. And they had put all the headstones in a heap somewhere promising to set them

all up again *tastefully* — he remembered — didn't matter
who was underneath. Bet there weren't any Maoris driving those bulldozers, well why to worry it's not his con-
cern, none of his whanaungas up there anyway.

Good those old trams but he didn't trust these crazy
buses, he'd rather walk. Besides he's nice and early and
there's nothing wrong with his legs. Yes, he knows this
place like his own big toe, and by Jove he's got a few
things to say to those people and he wasn't forgetting.
He'd tell them, yes.

The railway station was a place for waiting. People
waited there in the old days when times were hard, had
a free wash and did their starving there. He waited
because it was too early to go home, his right foot was
sore. And he could watch out for George, the others had
often seen George here waiting about. He and George
might go and have a cup of tea and some kai.

He agreed. Of course he agreed. People had to have
houses. Not only that, people had to have other
things — work, and ways of getting from place to place,
and comforts. People needed more now than they did in
his young days, he understood completely. Sir. Kept
calling him Sir, and the way he said it didn't sound so
well, but it was difficult to be sure at first. After a while
you knew, you couldn't help knowing. He didn't want
any kai, he felt sick. His foot hurt.

Station getting crowded and a voice announcing platforms. After all these years he still didn't know where
the voice came from but it was the same voice, and
anyway the trains could go without him it was too soon.
People.

Queueing for tickets and hurrying towards the platforms, or coming this way and disappearing out through
the double doors, or into the subway or the lavatory or

the cafeteria. He was too tired to go to the lavatory and anyway he didn't like ... . Some in no hurry at all. Waiting. You'd think it was starvation times. Couldn't see anyone he knew.

I know I know. People have to have houses, I understand and it's what I want.

Well it's not so simple Sir.

It's simple. I can explain. There's only the old place on the land and it needs bringing down now. My brother and sister and I talked about it years back. We wrote letters ... .

Yes yes but it's not as simple as you think.

But now they're both dead and it's all shared — there are my brother's children, my sister's children, and me. It doesn't matter about me because I'm on the way out, but before I go I want it all done.

As I say it's no easy matter, all considered.

Subdivison. It's what we want.

There'll be no more subdivision Sir, in the area.

Subdivision. My brother has four sons and two daughters, my sister has five sons. Eleven sections so they can build their houses. I want it all seen to before ... .

You must understand Sir that it's no easy matter, the area has become what we call a development area, and I've explained all this before, there'll be no more subdivision.

Development means houses, and it means other things too, I understand that. But houses, it's what we have in mind.

And even supposing Sir that subdivision were possible, which it isn't, I wonder if you fully comprehend what would be involved in such an undertaking.

I fully comprehend ... .

Surveying, kerbing and channelling and formation of

adequate access, adequate right of ways. The initial out-
lay . . . .

I've got money, my brother and sister left if for the
purpose. And my own, my niece won't use any of my
money, it's all there. We've got the money.

However that's another matter, I was merely pointing
out that it's not always all plain sailing.

All we want is to get it divided up so they can have a
small piece each to build on . . . .

As I say, the area, the whole area, has been set aside
for development. All in the future of course but we
must look ahead, it is necessary to be far-sighted in
these concerns.

Houses, each on a small section of land, it's what my
niece was trying to explain . . . .

You see there's more to development than housing.
We have to plan for roading and commerce, we have to
set aside areas for educational and recreational facilities.
We've got to think of industry, transportation . . . .

But still people need houses. My nieces and nephews
have waited for years.

They'd be given equivalent land or monetary com-
pensation of course.

But where was the sense in that, there was no equal
land. If it's your stamping ground and you have your
ties there, then there's no land equal, surely that wasn't
hard to understand. More and more people coming in to
wait and the plastic kids had arrived. They pulled away
from their mother and went for a small run, crackling.
He wished he knew their names and hoped they would
come and sit down by him, but no, their mother was
striding, turning them towards a platform because they
were getting a train home. Nothing to say for a week or
more and never wanted anything except sitting squeezed
beside him in the armchair after tea until he fell asleep.

Carry him to bed, get in beside him later then one day his mother would come. It was too early for him to go home even though he needed a pee.

There's no sense in it don't you see? That's their stamping ground and when you've got your ties there's no equal land. It's what my niece and nephew were trying to explain the last time, and in the letters . . . .

Well Sir I shouldn't really do this, but if it will help clarify the position I could show you what has been drawn up. Of course it's all in the future and not really your worry . . . .

Yes yes I'll be dead but that's not . . . .

I'll get the plans.

And it's true he'll be dead, it's true he's getting old, but not true if anyone thinks his eyes have had it because he can see good enough. His eyes are still good enough to look all over the paper and see his land there, and to see that his land has been shaded in and had 'Off Street Parking' printed on it.

He can see good close up and he can see good far off, and that's George over the other side standing with some mates. He can tell George anywhere no matter what sort of get-up he's wearing. George would turn and see him soon.

But you can't, that's only a piece of paper and it can be changed, you can change it. People have to live and to have things. People need houses and shops but that's only paper, it can be changed.

It's all been very carefully mapped out. By experts. Areas have been selected according to suitability and convenience. And the aesthetic aspects have been carefully considered . . . .

Everything grows, turnips the size of pumpkins, cabbages you can hardly carry, potatoes, tomatoes . . . . Back here where you've got your houses, it's all rock, land going to waste there . . . .

You would all receive equivalent sites . . . .

Resited . . . .

As I say on equivalent land . . . .

There's no land equal . . . .

Listen Sir, it's difficult but we've got to have some understanding of things. Don't we?

Yes yes I want you to understand, that's why I came. This here, it's only paper and you can change it. There's room for all the things you've got on your paper, and room for what we want too, we want only what we've got already, it's what we've been trying to say.

Sir we can't always have exactly what we want . . . .

All round here where you've marked residential it's all rock, what's wrong with that for shops and cars. And there'll be people and houses. Some of the people can be us, and some of the houses can be ours.

Sure, sure. But not exactly where you want them. And anyway Sir there's no advantage do you think in you people all living in the same area?

It's what we want, we want nothing more than what is ours already.

It does things to your land value.

He was an old man but he wanted very much to lean over the desk and swing a heavy punch.

No sense being scattered everywhere when what we want . . .

It immediately brings down the value of your land . . .

. . . is to stay put on what is left of what has been ours since before we were born. Have a small piece each, a small garden, my brother and sister and I discussed it years ago.

Straight away the value of your land goes right down.

Wanted to swing a heavy punch but he's too old for it. He kicked the desk instead. Hard. And the veneer cracked and splintered. Funny how quiet it had become.

You ought to be run in old man, do you hear.

Cripes look what the old blighter's gone and done. Look at Paul's desk.

He must be whacky.

He can't do that Paul, get the boss along to sort him out.

Get him run in.

Get out old man, do you hear.

Yes he could hear, he wasn't deaf, not by a long shot. A bit of trouble getting his foot back out of the hole, but there, he was going, and not limping either, he'd see about this lot later. Going, not limping, and not going to die either. It looked as though their six eyes might all fall out and roll on the floor.

There's no sense, no sense in anything, but what use telling that to George when George already knew sitting beside him wordless. What use telling George you go empty handed and leave nothing behind, when George had always been empty handed, had never wanted anything except to have nothing.

How are you son?

All right Uncle. Nothing else to say. Only sitting until it was late enough to go.

Going, not limping, and not going to die either.

There you are old man, get your feet in under that heater. Got her all warmed up for you.

Yes young fulla that's the story.

The weather's not so good.

Not the best.

How was your day all told?

All right.

It's all those hard footpaths, and all the walking that gives people sore feet, that's what makes your legs tired.

There's a lot of walking about in that place.

You didn't use the buses?

Never use the buses.

But you got your business done?

All done. Nothing left to do.

That's good then isn't it?

How's your day been young fulla?

A proper circus.

Must be this weather.

It's the weather, always the same in this weather.

This is your last trip for the day is it?

A couple of trains to meet after tea and then I finish.

Home to have a look at the telly.

For a while, but there's an early job in the morning . . . .

Drop me off at the bottom young fulla. I'm in no hurry. Get off home to your wife and kids.

No, no, there's a bad wind out there, we'll get you to your door. Right to your door, you've done your walking for the day. Besides I always enjoy the sight of your garden, you must have green fingers old man.

It keeps me bent over but it gives us plenty. When you come for Minnie on Tuesday I'll have a couple of cabbages and a few swedes for you.

Great, really great, I'm no gardener myself.

Almost too dark to see.

Never mind I had a good look this morning, you've got it all laid out neat as a pin. Neat as a pin old man.

And here we are.

One step away from your front door.

You can get off home for tea.

You're all right old man?

Right as rain young fulla, couldn't be better.

I'll get along then.

Tuesday.

Now he could get in and close the door behind him and walk without limping to the lavatory because he badly needs a pee. And when he came out of the bathroom they were watching him, they were stoking up the fire and putting things on the table. They were looking at his face.

Seated at the table they were trying not to look at his face, they were trying to talk about unimportant things, there was a bad wind today and it's going to be a rough night.

Tamatea Whakapau.

It must have been cold in town.

Heaters were on in the train.

And the train, was it on time?

Right on the minute.

What about the one coming home?

Had to wait a while for the one coming home.

At the railway station, you waited at the railway station?

And I saw George.

George, how's George?

George is all right, he's just the same.

Maisie said he's joined up with a gang and he doesn't wash. She said he's got a big war sign on his jacket and won't go to work.

They get themselves into trouble she said and they all go round dirty.

George is no different, he's just the same.

They were quiet then wondering if he would say anything else, then after a while they knew he wouldn't.

But later that evening as though to put an end to some

silent discussion that they may have been having he told them it wasn't safe and they weren't to put him in the ground. When I go you're not to put me in the ground, do you hear. He was an old man and his foot was giving him hell, and he was shouting at them while they sat hurting. Burn me up I tell you, it's not safe in the ground, you'll know all about it if you put me in the ground. Do you hear?

Some other time, we'll talk about it.

Some other time is now and it's all said. When I go, burn me up, no one's going to mess about with me when I'm gone.

He turned into his bedroom and shut the door. He sat on the edge of his bed for a long time looking at the palms of his hands.

Two

Kepa

Girls against boys today, and so there were the girls
with their dresses tucked into their pants, waiting. The
boys came out of their huddle and called, 'Ana.'
   'We call Ana.'
   'Ana Banana.'
   Ana could run it straight or try trickery. Straight she
decided, and committed now with a toe over the line.
Away with hair rippling, eyes fixed on the far corner,
that far far corner, the corner far . . . .
   Boys bearing down, slapping thighs and yodelling.
And confident. If Denny Boy didn't get her Macky
would.
   'Ana Banana.'
   'Anabanana.'
   'Banana Ana,' Denny Boy leaving the bunch in a fast
sprint, slowing down and lingering for the show of it,
then diving for the ankle slap. But not quite. Not quite.
Ana was ready for him. She side-stepped and kicked
him in the knee, then she was off again.
   Infield. No hope of a straight run now, nearly all on
top of her. Facing her. Spreading out and facing. Back
at the line the girls all screamed, 'Run Ana.'
   'Run.'
   'Ana run.'
   'Runana,' over the humps and cracks, plops and
thistles. Not far to go, but they all knew someone
would . . . Macky. She hit like a slammed door while
the other girls all yelled at her to get up Ana.

'Get up.'
'Up Ana.'
'Come on, gee.'
'Gee, come on Ana, get up.'
'Up.'

Macky's fingers were clamped to her ankle but he hadn't got her yet. He hadn't got her three times in the middle of the back and those were the rules. She kicked out with her free foot, but he wouldn't let go, and now the other boys were sitting on her. Thumping One, taking their time for the show of it, Two, caught Three. Howzat?

'Howzat?' The boys were doing some sort of dance, an arms and legs dance, a face dance, a bum dance, and the girls were wild. Sukeys they called.

'Pick a fast runner next time sukeys.'
'Cheats.'
'Sukeys and cheats.'

Not that the boys cared, getting together for their next conference. They decided to call Charlotte, just to prove they weren't sukeys. Or cheats.

'Cha-arlotte.'
'Ba-anjoes.'
'Charlotte Banjoes,' they weren't scared.

Charlotte leapt forward and three of the boys ran ahead to help from the front because they knew it would take a united effort. Macky was coming from behind, but suddenly Charlotte halted and put her foot out and he somersaulted over it. 'Go Charlotte, go Charlotte,' the girls screamed. She went off at another angle with only three boys to beat. She charged straight for them, stopped and buckled her knees at them, then changed direction again and went for the line. Safe, with Macky throwing dung at her and the girls yelling, 'All over, all over,' running out into the bunch of angry boys.

Two more of the girls ran across safely while those who were caught went to the sideline to recuperate, and to await the revenge time.

'How's that you fullas?'

'Only three of you fullas left.'

'Shut up you cheats.'

'Just only three.'

'Who do you call?'

Erana ran out with fists flying. She saw a little gap between Jack and Denny Boy that could be big enough for a side-step foot-change and through, but not quite. She was quickly caught, held and tagged, and so was Becky. That left Charlotte.

'Banjoes.'

'Cha-arlotte.'

'Ba-anjoes.'

Charlotte ran out on to the field and swerved round two of the boys. She knocked another down knowing there was still a long way to go. Knowing Macky had it in for her and that the foot trip wouldn't work a second time. He was gaining on her and wasn't put off by her sudden balk tactic. Still gaining, and with a strong group up front, Charlotte knew her chances were not good. She tried a change of direction but Macky stayed with her. He was close enough now but seemed to be delaying, and Charlotte didn't know why. Then suddenly she knew. She saw the thistle as Macky brought her down on top of it. Macky wisely held tightly on to both of her legs until help came. It came swiftly. 'One, Two, Three.'

'All out, all out.'

'Howzat?'

'Howzat you fullas?' but the girls were already conferring and Charlotte was enraged. 'Macky-Blacky,' she called, and she was going to throw that Macky in the tutae for sure.

After him. The slipperiest, the ugliest . . . . Charlotte was running alonside and they all knew she would have to do something quick because Macky-Blacky was faster than she was. She kicked his legs from under him and swiped him in the back with her fist. Macky was down with Charlotte on top of him. He wriggled on to his back so that she couldn't tag him; after all he was not only the fastest but also slipperiest so he wasn't caught yet. But Charlotte wasn't so interested in tagging him because there was a big round, soft plop not far away. She dug her knees into Macky's thighs, pinned his arms down and rolled. Now he was on top but still quite helpless. Another heave and roll . . . a splash and his back was right in it, good job. 'Good job Blacky.'

Macky bounced up, and suddenly there was blood pouring out of Charlotte's nose. Then the two of them were down again punching and kicking, while all the others shouted at them to get up.

'Come on, gee.'

'Gee-ee you're spoiling the game.'

'Gees you fullas spoil everything.'

And Denny Boy was really mad. He was still *in*. He hadn't been caught yet and these fullas must fight. He got through the fence and had a drink at the creek, then he sat on the stile to wait. Gee those two fighting, and the rest of them hopping about and shouting, and he was still *in*. He hadn't had his turn yet. A-ack they made him sick.

He stood up on the stile . . . and it was from there that he noticed, far away at the end of the beach where the road began, a little speck which seemed to roll from side to side. He'd seen that same speck doing that same thing more than two years ago. And he knew what it was if only he could remember — Now he remembered. He knew what it was, who it was. It was Uncle Kepa, home from the sea, lifting his feet high as he walked so as not to get dust on his shoes. Uncle Kepa who had been to all the countries in the world and who was bringing them back a monkey. Denny Boy began to run. Across the paddock, down to the beach and over the stones.

Back in mid-field Lizzie noticed him going for his life, he was cunning that Denny Boy. You had to watch Denny Boy, running off in the middle of a fight like that. He was up to something. Look at him, running like a porangi . . . .

'Uncle Kepa,' Lizzie screamed, and began to run too. The others were only seconds behind her, calling.

'Come back here Denny Boy.'

'Cheat.'

'Liar.'

'Stink bum.'

Charlotte, still running, ripped the bottom off her dress and wiped the blood from her face. Then she handed the rag to Macky who wiped all round his mouth where his teeth had come through his lip. 'You wait smarty,' she was yelling, 'Come back tutae face.' But Denny Boy was way ahead. Not even Macky or Charlotte could catch him now. And if Uncle Kepa gave that monkey to Denny Boy well watch out.

For some years now, whenever they had thought about Uncle Kepa who had been round the world thousands of times, millions of times and overcounting times, they would discuss claims on the pet monkey that their uncle would one day bring.

Charlotte said she should have it because she was the

eldest, but she would let them all come and see it whenever they wanted to. Denny Boy thought that he should be able to keep the monkey because he helped Uncle Kepa a lot. He cleaned Uncle's tank out, chopped his wood, and looked after his fishing lines while he was away. Becky and Lizzie backed Charlotte's claim because she was their sister and that would make them second in charge. One day Mereana had said that Uncle would be sure to give her the monkey because she was the youngest, and they all stared at her wondering if this could happen. No. Charlotte decided that Mereana was too small to look after a monkey.

Yes. The others were relieved. Mereana wasn't big enough but they would let her — and just then, Macky, who was stretched out on his back looking at the sky said, 'Uncle Kepa, he's going to give that monkey to me.'

'You?' they all yelled.

'You?'

'You don't even know Uncle Kepa.'

'You haven't even seen Uncle Kepa.'

'Aunty Connie, she only got you last year.'

'Uncle Kepa, he's not your real uncle.'

Macky closed his eyes, 'Uncle Kepa, I bet he'll give that monkey to me.'

'What for?'

'Yeah. What for? He never told you he was bringing a monkey.'

'You weren't here.'

'Aunty Connie, she only got you last year.'

'Uncle Kepa, he'll give that monkey to me.'

'What for?'

'Because I look like a monkey that's what for. And the monkey will like me the best.'

They all stared at Macky angrily, wondering. 'You always say that's what I look like, a monkey, so that means I do.' Macky got up and started running around on his hands and feet. Then he stood up, stuck his bottom teeth out up over his top lip and began scratching under his armpits. When he could see that they were really worried he ran up a tree and hung from a branch by one hand making noises like Tarzan's ape.

They watched him without speaking for a long time. Then Charlotte said, 'You don't look like a monkey any more.'

'No,' they all agreed. 'You don't look like a monkey at all.'

'Only when Aunty Connie first got you you did.'
But they were worried.

'I think Aunty Connie might give you back soon.' And after that they'd spent the rest of the morning swinging in the trees and gibbering.

Later that day someone had put forward the idea that if they made a house for the monkey and kept it in the orchard then that would be fair, because the orchard belonged to everyone. They had all agreed, each thinking he would find a way out if Uncle Kepa gave the monkey to him.

But now, there was Denny Boy hugging Uncle Kepa. And while it was one thing to be the eldest, or the youngest, or to be lucky and look like a monkey, it was another thing to be first and *smart*. Uncle Kepa was sitting himself down in the lupins at the side of the road to wait for them. He put his arms out and they all fell in.'Ah my babies, my babies,' he kept saying.

His babies all hugged him then moved back so the monkey wouldn't get squashed. Where would Uncle keep a monkey? So far they couldn't see a monkey anywhere. All Uncle's pockets were flat and he wasn't carrying any boxes. There was only his bag. Charlotte dug her elbow into Mereana and whispered, 'You ask, you're the youngest.' So Mereana hid behind Lizzie. And Denny Boy, making sure to keep the upper hand said, 'Uncle you got us a monkey?'

'Ah no my babies. Not this time. The monkey, he got away. That monkey, he's too quick for this funny old uncle. Next time my babies.'

Ah well.

They walked along the beach with their uncle who rolled from side to side as though he was still on board. Uncle was a big strong man, and he had chased a monkey the length and breadth of some faraway jungle, climbing trees and swinging from branch to branch, but the monkey had got away. It shows you how quick and clever monkeys are.

That evening when Uncle Kepa was sitting in a chair by the stove at Aunty Connie's place with all the kids hanging round, he said, 'Ah that's good. Good to be a landlubber for a while. Good to see all my babies again. All my babies. These the only babies I got.' Then the kids heard Aunty Connie say, 'What about that drop kick of yours over in Aussie?' and Aunty Connie was laughing.

Then Uncle looked at the ceiling and started to laugh too, 'Ee hee, ee hee, ee hee hee.' Uncle Kepa was a great big man but his laugh was high and skinny like a seagull noise. And gee they all had a lot of things to talk about when it was time to go back to school. All about their uncle who was a great big man who went everywhere in the world in a big ship. And who was bringing them a monkey one day. As well as that they'd just found out that uncle was a famous footballer too, and it made him laugh like anything.

The Pictures

After all she and Ana wore shoes to the pictures now, and hers had the toes and heels out, and she'd been promised stockings for the winter. 'I might get me some earrings,' she said to Ana, as though earrings grew on trees.

They'd spent most of the afternoon getting themselves ready for the pictures, heating the irons on the stove and going over the skirts and blouses — pressing and steaming, reheating and pressing. Then they'd taken the basins outside and washed their hair, and now they sat on the stile waiting for it to dry. 'And I might get me a haircut,' Ana said. Charlotte drew in her breath, 'Ana, we wouldn't be allowed.'

'Yes, well. I might get me a haircut anyway — and I'm putting mine up for tonight.'

'So am I.'

'Let's go and try it now. See if it suits us. You do mine and I'll do yours.'

In front of the bedroom mirror with clips and elastic. Charlotte pulling the wire brush through her hair. Pounding the brush on to her scalp, dragging it down through the layers of thick tangles. Scraping up now, and out, up and out. Until the room is filled with flying streamers of Charlotte's hair.

Ana spread the circle of elastic on her fingers and worked carefully, putting the ends of Charlotte's hair into the band. She let the band close, then tied a ribbon tightly over the band and pulled the bundle of hair up

and under at the back of Charlotte's neck. She spread
the fold so that it rested thickly about Charlotte's shoulders. A clip above each ear to hold the hair in place.
Finished.

Charlotte looked into the mirror smoothing and pat-
ting. Not bad. Not too bad. As long as the elastic would
stay, as long as the clips would hold. Ana was hover-
ing, 'It suits you. It does. It suits you.' 'Ye-es. Not
bad. Not too bad.' Charlotte could see Macky and
Denny Boy peeping round the open door at her but she
couldn't be bothered with them, not with her hair done
up, and it suiting her. She arched her eyebrows and
stroked her hair, 'Get those kids out Ana,' she sighed.
'Get those nosey brats out.'

'Get out,' said Ana, making a face and slamming the
door. 'We don't want any kids hanging round—Yes, it
suits you Charlotte.'

'It's O.K. Course when I get dressed up. With the
skirt . . . and shoes . . . . I'll do yours now. Then we'll
go, over to Linda's and do hers and tonight we'll wear
some old boots on to the road to keep our shoes clean.'

'Are those kids still hanging round?'

Ana opened the door. 'They've gone,' she said.

The boys had wanted it to be a cowboy one but it was
going to be a sloppy one after all, with kissing and people singing — La la la . . . .

'La la la,' Macky sang with one hand on his heart
and the other extended to his love Denny Boy. 'La la la,
will you marry me?'

'No,' Denny Boy sang. 'No I won't my darling.'

'Thank you. La la la . . . .'

'Anyway,' said Denny Boy, flopping down on to his
stomach, 'we mightn't be going yet.'

'We'll go. We'll get there.'

'Aunty Connie won't give us any money. I just walked over her scrubbed floor — by accident. Just by accident.'

'What did she do?'

'Picked up her mop. So I took off. She's in a bad mood. For nothing.'

'We better not ask her for any.'

'No . . . .'

'What about Uncle Harry?'

'He's too mingy.'

'We could hoe his garden for him, and chop his morning wood.'

'Boy we'd be working all day.'

'And he mightn't give us anything. He might be broke.'

'And we might work all day for nothing.'

'Let's go and see Aunty Myra then.'

'O.K. she might.'

'But she mightn't.'

'But she might.'

And there was Aunty scratching her borders with the rake and all her ducks scrummaging into the loose soil at her feet. Wonder what sort of mood she's in.

'Hello Aunty.'

'Tena koe Denny Boy.' Talking Maori ay? Must be in a good mood — not like that Aunty Connie.

'Hello Aunty.'

'Tena koe e hoa. Kei te pehea korua?'

'Kei te pai Aunty.' Talk Maori back to her.

'Yeh. Kei te pai Aunty.' That'll keep her in a good mood.

'Ka pai.'

'We came over to see you.'

'To see how you're getting on with your flowers.'

'And your ducks.'

'Ka pai ano. Kei whea o korua hoa?'

'Down the beach.' Hope that's right.

'Yes down the beach. And Charlotte and Ana are do-dahing themselves up for the pictures.'

'The pictures tonight.'

'Ah.'

'It's a good one.'

'Yes real good.'

'Kei te haere korua?'

'Not him. Not me, but all those others are going. Everyone else.'

'But him and me, we can't go.'

'Na te aha?'

'Because . . . because . . . Aunty Connie's in a bad mood. For nothing.'

'Yes just for nothing.'

'Kare aku moni e tama ma.'

And that's easy enough to understand, she's bloody well broke.

Shit what a waste of a good mood . . . .

'Well . . . .'

'Well . . . we have to go Aunty. I hope your flowers are all right.'

'And your ducks.'

'Haere ra e hoa ma.'

Uncle Harry was hoeing up the dirt round his kumara plants. They could see him from the willows at the back of his place.

'All that and he might be broke, like Aunty Myra.'

'Wait a bit longer. When he gets to the last two rows we'll go and help.'

'If he's broke we'll have to try to get Aunty Connie in a good mood.'

'That's too hard.'

'Mmm. Worse than hoeing up Uncle's kumara.'

'All this trouble and it's only a sloppy love one.'

'Yes. La la la . . . .'

'Shut up, he'll hear.'

'Anyway he's nearly finished. Let's go and help.'

'Hello Uncle. We came to help you hoe up your kumara.'

'Hello boys. Good on you. Get another hoe from the shed and one of you can have this one. I'll sit down and have a smoke. You two can be the workers and I'll be the boss.'

He sat down and began shredding tobacco along his paper as the boys started to mound the dirt up under the vines.

'That's the way boys. Heap them up. When we dig them there'll be plenty for you to take home.' Well it wasn't a bag of kumara they wanted.

'Plenty of potatoes too.' Or spuds.

'Those others are playing down the beach Uncle.'

'Yes they're lazy.'

'Just playing. But Macky and I, we like to come and help you with your garden.'

'Instead of playing.'

'That's good boys. Keep it up. Careful of those vines.'

'After this we'll chop your morning wood for you.'

'That's the way. Good on you mates.'

'. . . Uncle?'

'Ay?'

'You know what Charlotte and them are doing?'

'No.'

'Looking at their ugly selves in the mirror.'

'And ironing their clothes.'

'Ironing their clothes ay?'

'They think they're bea-utiful like ladies in the pictures.'

'And their hair is all done up funny like rags.'

'And they got banjo feet and gumboot lips, but they think they look bea-utiful, la la la . . . .'

'Hey Uncle.'

'Ay?'

'You know why Charlotte and them are ironing their clothes and washing their hair?'

'No.'

'They're going to the pictures.'

'Ah the pictures. What's on tonight?'

'Well it's a good one . . . a cowboy one.'

'Yes a good cowboy one Uncle . . . . All those lazy kids are going.'

'All of them ay?'

'Yes all.'

'Well boys you've done a good job there.'

What was the matter with Uncle Harry? Wasn't he listening? They'd hoed up two rows of kumara and now they were lopping the dry brush heads off the manuka and tying it into a bundle to start his stove in the morning. They'd told Uncle that all those lazy kids were going to the pictures but he wasn't listening.

'Good, good. Put your hoes away in the shed now, and stick our axe in the block.' Was he deaf or something?

'Got any more jobs Uncle?'

'No that's all boys.' Deaf all right. No ears. All that hoeing, all that chopping. And old Uncle No Ears going up his steps and in his door . . . .

'See you later Uncle.' Deaf Ears.

'O.K. boys. Hey don't you want these?'

Up on to the verandah, pecking the coins from Uncle's big dried paua of a hand. Running, shouting. Shouting . . . .

'Thank you Uncle.'

'Thank you.'
'La la la.'
'La la la.'

Lizzie was coughing again. Mereana ran with her down the track past the garden, Lizzie's eyes bulging like two turnips, her chook hand clawed over her mouth. Running into the dunny and banging the door. Then the coughing. Mereana kept watch outside because they wouldn't let Lizzie go to the pictures tonight if they knew she had her cough.

And from where Mereana waited, she could hear the cough gurgling and rumbling up Lizzie's throat then barking out of her mouth as though Lizzie was a dog. Then after a while the gurgling and rumbling and barking stopped and she could hear Lizzie spitting down the dunny hole.

Coming out now with the bottom half of her face all white and stretched and her pop eyes watery and pink. 'Come down the beach,' Lizzie gasped at her. 'So they won't hear.'

Down through the lupins with the black pods busting, which was nothing really, only a sound. Laying on the beach stones and licking them for salt. Lizzie gurgling and squeaking, and Lizzie was nothing but an old crumpled bit of paper there beside her. What if Lizzie died right now?

'Lizzie, Lizzie! There'll be a lot of kissing I bet.'
'Mmm. Plenty . . . of kissing.'
'And she'll have lovely dresses, Lizzie.'
'Yes . . . .'
'The men will fight over her. Ay?'
'Mmm.'
'But the best one will marry her.'
'Mmm. At . . . the end.'

'And they'll have a long long kiss.'

'At the end.'

Bending over the sea now. Her neck stretched and lumpy like a sock full of stones. Spitting on the water. 'Don't cough Lizzie,' Mereana called. 'Don't. They'll hear you. They'll make you stay home.'

Oh but it wasn't that. Not the staying home. The cough was too big. Bigger than the sea — bigger than the sky. Now standing up, pulling a big breath in, 'Yes... I bet she has... lovely dresses.' And another long breath. In. 'There'll be a long long kiss... at the end... I bet.'

At the gate where the road began, Charlotte, Ana and Linda took off their old shoes and hid them in the lupins, then carefully slid their feet into the good shoes and smoothed the skirts, patted the hair. Ahead of them the others were running along the sea wall yelling. Leaping down on to the sand, running back up the wall, but they were only kids. They didn't want kids hanging round. Mereana and Lizzie dawdling along behind them and that Lizzie barking her head off. 'We'll sit up the back,' Charlotte said, 'so we won't have *kids* hanging round.'

Not that the others wanted to anyway. Charlotte, Ana and Linda stank and had canoes for shoes and rags for hair. What's more, Charlotte and them, they had hairs under their arms and they were growing tits as well, just like cows. Along the top of the sea wall, flying now, and landing in sand. Cold. Sand goes dead at night time, up the wall again. Bits of shell everywhere, winking, on the road getting blacker every minute.

And waiting. At the store waiting. Lollies and a drink, then up the verandah poles, swinging and sliding — except for stinky Charlotte and them. Not

Lizzie and Mereana either, Lizzie coughing like an old goat and baby Mereana nearly crying. Then . . . .

'Here it comes.'

'Here it comes.'

Two eyes rounding the corner, bowling downhill. Jack had his foot down tonight.

Slowing down. Stopping.

'At last.'

'Yes. At last.'

Money in the tin. Smart the way Jack flicks you the ticket.

But Charlotte, Ana and Linda were waiting till last. What was the hurry? Damn kids. Always in a hurry. Always pushing. Always in the way. Well . . . well . . . . Might as well get in.

'Might as well get in you two.'

'Might as well.'

'Go on then.'

'No you.'

'You first.'

'Go *on*'.

Up the steps. Gum rolling, eyes down. Wondering who's staring. All those big eyes in the bus must stare — or were they? Have a look, look away. They knew it, people *were* staring.

'All looking pretty tonight aincha?' Jack yelled.

Bloody Jack. And now that Ana. That Ana had started giggling. Charlotte and Linda were wild with her. No wonder everyone was staring. No wonder . . . . And look at Linda. Now Linda was going to. Sneaking along the bus with her hand up over her mouth, snorting behind her hand. Gee they made Charlotte wild those two — and Jack. Everyone staring.

Now Linda was looking at her with cow's eyes, rolling her fat eyes at her and cackling like a chook. Then oh! Oh shame. She, Charlotte, could feel all the little dribbles of laughter gathering in her throat — climbing, pushing . . . . Pushing. She threw herself on to the seat between Ana and Linda as the sounds fizzed and exploded behind her hand.

The boys who had sat behind the girls at the pictures got off the home bus at the store and followed the girls along the beach road. They were tossing bits of shell into the girls' hair and shoving each other. The girls were giggling and telling each other secrets. Those kids were going to get a good hiding too, running up and down the sea wall. Shouting, 'Give them a kiss.'

'Kiss.'

'Kiss, kiss.'

'Kiss, kiss, kiss.'

Making sure to keep out of Charlotte's way because she wasn't really a beautiful lady you know. You had to watch Charlotte for the left hook and the leg trip, yes.

Ack those big boys were dumb following Charlotte and them. Whistling between their teeth and chucking things.

'Give them a kiss.'

'A kiss.'

'La la la.'

But no. No kiss. The boys had stopped now that they had come to the end of the road, and they were calling out to the girls.

But Charlotte, Ana and Linda weren't answering. They had remembered something and were walking ahead, not talking, not turning, not looking down . . . .

Their hair suited them

Their skirts suited them.

They had shoes to wear to the pictures.

They might be getting earrings.

And stockings.

And haircuts.

And they'd just remembered.

And now Macky and Denny Boy had remembered too. 'Hey you girls. What about your old boots you hid in the lupins?'

'Your old pakaru boots.'

Then away for their lives over the dark paddocks, through the thistles and plops. Lucky they had a head start. Up over the stile and jump the creek. Lucky they could see in the dark, those smartheads would never get them now — across the yard and in. Canoes for shoes. Rags for hair. Not till tomorrow. They'd kill them tomorrow.

But that's tomorrow.

Yes.

Drifting

They were up while it was still dark, running through the wet lupins with the tin of herrings, over the black stones to Uncle Kepa's hut. There they put the tin under the step, pushed the door open and went in.

Still asleep. But his morning wood was ready on the hearth. Mereana opened the grate and put the wood in on top of the crumpled newspaper. She lit the fire and moved the kettle over. Lizzie was mixing porridge.

'Hello my babies. You got our bait?'

'Yes Uncle. Plenty herrings.'

'Stoke up then. Your funny uncle will get changed.'

They heard him moving around in his other room, then he went outside and filled his basin at the tank-stand. Uncle. He had a wash for going fishing, but just as well she and Lizzie hadn't wasted any time washing this morning or brushing their hair. Just as well they'd slept in their clothes to make sure about being early, because Uncle had forgotten to wake up. Get up, straighten the blankets, out over the verandah and away.

Now Lizzie was spooning porridge into three enamel plates.

'Come on Uncle,' Mereana called.

He came in making the room small. The skin on his face was mottled with the shock of cold water. His eyelids were rimmed with red as though his eyes had been always shut and forgotten but had now suddenly been slit open with a sharp blade to reveal surprised and bulging brown eyes, the whites all yellowed with waiting. His lashes, too, seemed as though they had this minute been put there, standing stiff and straight like glued bristles.

Mostly Uncle's face was long and thin, with big folds of skin hanging down, but his cheekbones were round and jutting. His nose was hooked at the tip, with a big bubble of flesh at either side. He wore the top half of a football jersey with the bottom half of a black singlet sewn on to it; and he carried a billy of milk which he had brought in from the outside safe.

The room swung back to its normal size as he sat down, and there was a grey light coming in through the one little window high up in the wall. Uncle Kepa leaned over his dish and stuck his bottom lip way out like a shelf, then rested the spoon with the hot porridge there and sucked. The spoonful of porridge was gone.

'Ah. Ah good my babies.'

Mereana stopped staring at her uncle and began pouring tea while Lizzie ran to rescue the bread that was toasting by the grate.

The little bit of dirty sea in the bottom of the dinghy swung and eddied with each push. Then away, rocketing down over the stones until the bow crunched into sand at the tip of the water. One more big push and it was flying out into the lagoon with Mereana and Lizzie throwing themselves in over its sides. Uncle Kepa, who had rolled his trousers up and whose legs were *white*, stepped in over the back and sat down on the middle seat to take up the oars.

They were soon through the channel, pulling out over the belt of brown kelp where the sea changed to a dull navy blue, then further still to where the water became thick and green.

The day was alight now. Far away, back on the

shore, the sun was sending silver off the roofs of all the tiny houses, and streamers of smoke leaned from the morning chimneys. As they rounded the point they could see the large patches of brown rock below them in the water, while rocks closer to land and not yet warmed and browned by the touch of sun stood black with the cold of night on them, and at their feet was a white lacework of smashed sea.

Out on the water, so far away that it was like being nowhere and like being no one, where even Uncle Kepa wasn't big any more, they let the rope down with the bag of stones on it and began baiting their hooks. Mereana watched her sinker break the surface and felt it take her line deep down into the sea. Who would be first? She could see a few feet of line before it disappeared, and could feel a small tingling. A quick glance at Lizzie. Lizzie was looking into the water too. Wondering perhaps who would be first. Thinking perhaps about all the fish in all the sea in all the world . . . .

One of them will get on my line. I will pull it up quickly, and I will be first . . . . Who would? Uncle Kepa was leaning forward with elbows on his knees. And gee. Uncle Kepa, he was asleep. What if a big fish got on Uncle's line and he didn't know? What if a shark came and bit the boat in half; who would save them? And if an albatross as big as the one in the museum came and took her and Lizzie away, who would fight it? Mereana forgot her line for the moment.

'Lizzie, Uncle's asleep.'

But then Uncle's hand with the line in it shot up above his head. His eyes popped open and he began to pull in. Uncle was first. Mereana and Lizzie watched him bring in his tarakihi then went back to their fishing.

'I got one. I got one Uncle. I got one Mereana.' Liz-

zie's face was all red and she was zipping her line up.
Now Lizzie had a fish and Mereana didn't. She could
feel some little nibbles on her line but the fish kept
going away and getting on Lizzie's and Uncle Kepa's.
Perhaps she was on the wrong side.

'Change seats Lizzie.' But Lizzie wouldn't. She
knew the good side. Lizzie used to be her best cousin
and her best . . . . Got one!

'I got one Uncle. I got one Lizzie.'

Hand over hand, hand over hand. Watching in the
water. Far down a shadow moving, coming closer.
There was her fish. Nearly to the top. Waving in the
water like a big shiny hand.

Then, as the fish broke the surface her line went
slack. The shadow that had been her fish was speeding
back to the deep.

'Never mind baby. Catch another one soon.'

And there was Lizzie who used to be her best friend
pulling in another one. It didn't get away from Lizzie
either.

Never mind. They were there again. Nibbling, pulling, snatching. And if only the boat would keep still
for a while, or was it herself? Just her, going up and
down, up and down? The sun was above them now
bouncing its heat at them from off the surface of the
water. And the sea. The sea was rocking them from side
to side. Up and back, up and back . . . . Uncle had tied
his line to a rowlock. He was taking some old crayfish
out that he had brought for bait.

'Waste of good crayfish,' he was saying. 'Waste giving it to the fish.'

He snapped the legs and began sucking the rotting
flesh from them. Suck. Suck.

'Waste of good crayfish for those fish down there,'
he said. 'Waste of good kai.'

Something was wrong with Mereana. Her stomach was all pinched up and she had no spit left. 'Up and back, up and back,' said the sea. The sun was going on and off and she could hear Uncle saying, 'Put your head over baby. Put your head over,' so she did. Her throat was stretching out wide. And there she was, sicking on to the sea. She watched the sick floating away like a little white nest on the water.

But what was Uncle doing? Pulling in the anchor.

'No Uncle.'

She wiped her mouth on the bottom of her dress.

'No Uncle. I want to catch one. A fish. A fish Uncle.' Letting it down. Letting the anchor down.

'A little while, a little while,' he was saying. Well that's good. That's all right. Her line tinkled and rang, then suddenly it swam away.

'I got one. Got one, see.' She pulled quickly.

'Got one Uncle. Got one Lizzie.' She could see it now nearly at the top. Don't get away. Bigger than Lizzie's. Bigger than Uncle Kepa's. And Uncle Kepa, he was leaning over the side with a gaff hook. Don't . . . .

Her line was empty again. She saw her fish flip and dive. Then.

Then there was a great crashing in the water and the sea had turned white. It had Uncle in it.

'Uncle!'

Uncle Kepa's head popped out of the water.

'I got it baby.' And he held up the gaff with her fish flapping and gasping on it. Her fish. And it was bigger than Lizzie's. Bigger than Uncle's.

He reached over the side and put the gaff with the fish on it into the boat. He turned the boat and took hold of the anchor rope and began easing himself up. Uncle was brave you know. What if a shark came and bit his legs off, or a whale, or a giant octopus like the one that picked up a whole submarine in the pictures. The back of the boat rose as he levered himself up over the bow. He was in. He made it and his legs were still on.

The back of the boat came down with a slap and a wave whacked against its side and splashed in.

'Bail out mates.'

Mereana and Lizzie took the bailing tins and began throwing the wave back.

'We got it Uncle. We got my fish.'

'We got it baby. We got that big fulla.' He was pulling up the anchor now. Never mind.

'These funny fishermen are all wet,' he said.

Out from the point they watched him take his spinner from his fishing bag. He tied the end of the line to the back seat and straightened the boat for a hard pull homeward. Then they were shinning out over the water, which now that they had rounded the corner was quiet and unruffled in a windless afternoon. Mereana watched the spinner sending out a fine white spray behind them. Would they catch a kahawai as Uncle said. Because fish don't eat paua shells.

'Uncle, kahawai don't eat paua shells.'

With each big pull Uncle Kepa's breath was hissing out between his teeth, 'The kahawai . . . he think . . . it . . . a herring.' Gee Uncle. Anyone could see it was a paua shell with holes in it spinning on a line. Most of the time Uncle was clever and strong, and he could row fast, and he had jumped in the sea and saved her fish. But now . . . Uncle thought . . . .

The kahawai struck. There was a green-silver flash, and spray ribboned up and out as the boat dragged the fish through the water.

'We got one. We got one. The kahawai he thought it was a herring. Gee he thought the bit of paua shell was herring. Dumb ay Lizzie? Dumb ay Uncle?'

'Dumb ay Mereana.'

The lagoon was full of children, waiting to see how good the catch had been.

Mereana and Lizzie were tired that night. They had been up early and out fishing. So many things had happened that the other kids hadn't believed them. They lay side by side on Lizzie's little bed. It was a warm night. They could hear the sea scrambling up the stones.

'Mereana?'

'What?'

'I wonder where your sick is.'

'Something might've ate it.' Because fish were dumb. They didn't know one thing from another.

'I think it's still there on the water.'

But Mereana was tired. Her eyes closed. Away, away, in a dark place far at the back of her eyes there was a little nest drifting . . . . Drifting. Somewhere far away on a dark, dark sea . . . .

Whitebait

At most times of the year the creek kept its secrets to itself. In the armpits of its banks eels tucked themselves, and outsized worms made quiet, intricate passages. Brown trout and cockabullies fed against the creek's knobbled belly. And the transients — larvae of dragon, damsel and may fly — waited for the time when they would climb out into air and fly away.

But at this time of the year the creek abandoned secrecy, and as though parting great legs and giving sudden and copious birth, set crowds of whitebait speeding for the sea.

The children had made a net from an old petticoat that Aunty Connie had given them, and they ran with it to the creek. They put the net down in a narrow place facing upstream. The net ballooned in the water, and Denny Boy from up-creek called, 'Coming.' He began to wade towards them, swishing his shoo-shie stick from bank to bank and watching the whitebait race ahead of him.

As he got close to the net the whitebait at the head of the shoal began to turn, trying to escape. But there was no escape. He directed them expertly into the net's open mouth.

Macky and Charlotte lifted the net and took it up on to the bank where they emptied the whitebait into a tin. Then they moved further up-creek to where the water was still clear, to set the net down again.

Later in the morning Lizzie and Mereana were sent back to Aunty Connie's for some eggs and fat and a frying pan. They waited in the willows not far from the house wondering what they should do.

'I think,' said Mereana, 'if we ask her she might . . . .'

'But if she's in a mood,' said Lizzie, 'we'll get a flick on the ear and a job to do.'

Just then the door of the house opened and their aunty came out with a bucket of water, a scrubbing brush and a block of sandsoap, and went round to the front of the house.

'She's in a mood,' whispered Mereana. 'I saw her face.'

'She's in a mood all right,' Lizzie agreed.

'So?'

'You get the pan and the fat, I'll get the eggs.'

Run.

To the outside safe.

To the hen house.

Then walk quickly back to the hiding willows with the pan and the fat.

Quiet chookies, quiet. You know me ay, I'm Lizzie. I gave you plenty wheat this morning, tons and tons. And plenty water. Sh-sh chookies.

Take the eggs quietly.

Shut the hen house door. Carefully. And turn the nailed block into position to make sure the door stays shut.

Get behind the hen house and breathe. Breathe out holding the warm eggs gently.

They could hear Aunty Connie bashing the front steps with her scrubbing brush.

The others had made a fireplace and collected dry rushes and sticks, and now they were in the creek

again, lifting stones to find crayfish. When Mereana and
Lizzie returned, Denny Boy got out of the water and lit
the fire. Charlotte washed a stick, strained the water
away from the whitebait, whipped the eggs in with them
and cooked them in the pan. Macky put fresh water into
one of the tins and put the koura on to cook as well.

Pin eyes and pinchers.

They'd never know what a bright colour they had
become.

And how many eyes could a panful of whitebait
have?

Not one pair of eyes now that would see the sea.

Eyes. Aunty Connie never saw.

Out front banging her steps.

Pull away the pink shells and toss them on the fire.

Hang the hot flesh on your tongue.

Let it burn.

The only way to taste.

To know.

Is to let it burn.

Bite the eyed heads and there's more to know.

Knowing the creek and wind sounds, and the small
one-eyed glow that is the fire, the hiding willows and
nailed wood block on the hen house door. And the
cocked hen eye, and the lifted curled foot of a hen.

Knowing the whipped bleeding cuts that the cutty
grass has made on legs and arms, and remembering a
woman with a scrubbing bucket pounding the front
steps, back on to the drumming sea.

Suddenly all is made small and known, fitting easily
on the tongue before being swallowed with a quick,
cooling breath.

Denny Boy took out his tin of cigarette butts and tipped
them on to the ground. He unwrapped each one and

teased the collection of tobacco evenly along an oblong of brown paper, then rolled his cigarette slowly using the tips of his fingers and thumbs. They were all watching him. He half shut his eyes and spat carefully on the edge of the paper and rubbed the spit along with his finger.

Charlotte had left her tin behind, in a tree in the orchard. So had Macky and Ana, under the floor in the shed.

Denny Boy smoothed the wet edge of the paper down, leaned into the eye of the fire and lit up.

They watched him draw in and let the smoke out holding the cigarette finely between the very tips of two fingers.

They watched him blowing out with his eyes half shut. And pulling his cheeks in.

Puffing out between lips that were formed into a little circle.

'Give us one.'

'There's no more.'

They watched him lay back and blow dawdling smoke into the trees.

Shoo-shie sticks.

And cigarette butts.

He was King, and as he closed his eyes he heard the others stamping off through the bush to look for thistle. Huh.

Anybody knew dried thistle wouldn't light up properly.

Anybody knew it gave you a mouth ache.

Butts and sticks.

Whitebait and koura.

And smoke going easily into the trees.

When the cigarette was half gone he pinched the lit end off, and put it away in his pocket. And later when the others had come back with their thistle stalks and huffed and gasped, and hurt their mouths, and made their throats sore. Then. That was when he would find the other half of the cigarette in his pocket.

And he'd light it and draw in, and hold smoke in him for a long long time, and his half shut eyes would see them watch. He'd blow out slowly.

Slow and

Blow.

He could hear them somewhere behind him, treading through the rushes.

Kip

The old hall was as accommodating as trees. On the way home from school, and when they were younger, the kids would stop and bounce their bald tennis balls against its wall — sevensies to onesies, right hand, left hand, whirls and claps. They planted their feet on it doing against-the-wall handstands, their eyes dropping from their heads. The recessed doorway was a ghost house, a witch hole, a tick-a-lock home base.

Dogs sniffed the bottom edges of the building before lifting a leg. Sparrows and starlings scrabbled and fluttered in the spoutings and corrugations, and when the time was right made their nests. It was the birds, dogs, and kids that gave the hall its animal smell.

But, while the outside of the animal retained its spots — grey and white dried splashes left by season after season of bird, flat black pennies made by the bouncing balls, patches of dog dribble, and the smeared footprints with toes pointing earthwards — the inside now had a new look. The walls had been painted pale blue. The old stage had new blue satin curtains, and new facings, painted white and edged in blue glitter. The leaking roof had been mended and the ceiling strung with twisted streamers of pink, white, and blue crepe paper. From the centre of the ceiling hung the blue moon.

On weekdays with the door shut and no light or sound coming from within, it was still the 'old hall', but on Saturdays it had become the 'Blue Moon' dance hall. And on those nights once the lights went on and the doorman was ready with his tin and his roll of tickets the band would string out its first few notes, and the turning mirrored ball would be spotlighted in blue. Then the floor would quickly fill with dancers all measled with moving blue light.

Bob gave an uneasy lead, striding deep into the corners and not knowing quite how to come out of them again. His arm about her waist exerted no pressure, and the cupped hand in which she placed hers could just as easily have been holding one of the hairless tennis balls they'd kicked goals with, or chucked again and again against walls.

'Apprentice electrician,' he said. 'With my old man.'

'Do you like it?'

'I like it okay. What about you, what're you doing?'

'I'll be leaving school at the end of the year.'

'Then what?'

'Don't know. I might go nursing.'

'You like it all right do you? School I mean.'

'I'm sick of it. Glad this is my last year.'

'I really hated school. Couldn't get away quick enough myself.'

And just then Mereana had a sudden picture of him at seven years of age standing in front of the class wearing a white shirt and a pair of navy shorts, his fair hair oiled into the shape of a shell. His face was entranced, and shocking to look at, and a sudden stream of pee was running down his leg.

Now after remembering that, it was difficult to speak: he had noticed her shift of memory. 'The band's all right,' she said.

'I hear they're having a singer later on.'

'Probably the same one they had last week.'

'She's all right too.'

His legs at seven years of age had been thin and veiny.

As Lizzie danced past, the blue light turned the red spots on her cheeks to purple. Reuben Hails' large hand on her waist moved her first away then close as they toed round the floor. Looking at Reuben, Mereana could read the contempt that Lizzie was too close to see, and which in any case she had never learned to see. Lizzie's large eyes, fringed by large curled back lashes, rested like two sea anemones just above Reuben's shoulder.

'Your cousin and Reuben are hitting it off,' Bob said to her.

'Lizzie.'

'Yes. I don't remember her so well.'

'She missed quite a lot of school.'

'She was sick a lot wasn't she?'

'Yes but she's okay now, or supposed to be.' (Her lung was 'cured' — like salted pork.) 'Do you know Reuben well?'

'He's older. Used to be in my brother's class. He thinks the sun shines out of his arse.'

It was a long speech for him. She liked Bob, who had no questions behind the eyes, no hidden slivers of glass in the cupped hand, and the light and shadows spinning across his face came only from the turning spot-lit ball. Mereana put her hand into the triangle that he'd made with his arm as the music frittered away, and he led her to her seat.

'Bob. Bob-ee,' Macky sang in her ear as she sat down beside him. 'La-la-la.'

'Give us a cig,' she said.

He drew in on the cigarette that he was smoking, then passed it to her. 'Last one,' he said. Reuben's elbow crushed Lizzie's hand to his side as he walked her towards them. Macky put his head back and blew smoke balls towards the ceiling. 'Reuben Hails,' he said, 'has got a theory . . . about dark skinned women . . . .' Reuben turned to Lizzie, twitched the corners of his mouth, and walked quickly away. 'Did you know?'

'You can guess it easy enough,' Mereana said.

'What're you talking about?' Lizzie asked. She was breathless.

'Throw your eyes in there,' Macky said nodding towards the supper room. 'Sausage rolls, cakes, sandwiches. Food,' he hooted. 'When are we going to have food?'

'Just watch out for Reuben,' Mereana said to Lizzie.

Charlotte and Denny Boy came over. 'I think the next one's going to be the supper waltz,' Charlotte said.

The sea spread beside them like a length of tossed shot silk. The old bus sailed the sea's curve, its headlights catching the white tips of the waves.

When they got off the bus they could hear the sea niggling at the shore stones, then there was the skirr of sprayed road metal above the grind of the gear changes as the bus backed, turned, and rocked away in the dark. They lifted a hand to Bob whose face and hand appeared briefly at the back window. She liked Bob whose eyes held no questions. The kiss in the bus had made no demands, had taken away nothing apart from a small breath.

'They shouldn't have gone with him,' Lizzie was saying.

'Don't worry about them,' Mereana said. 'Anyway we said to you to watch out . . . .'

'I know.'

'Why did you then?'

'Well he said only for a minute. Then when we walked along . . . .'

'He wanted to get you in under the trees with him.'

'He got all funny when I wouldn't . . . .'

'It's because of his theory,' Macky said to the stars.

'Anyhow what about Charlotte? She was dancing round with him. Smiling and all that, after I came back and told yous what had happened.'

'Don't worry about Charlotte.'

'What's on anyway? Where've they gone?'

'Some sort of party up at Ian and them's place.'

Then as they came nearer to the home gate they heard singing and saw that all the lights were on at their Aunty Connie's place. They began to hurry, over the stile and over the plank across the creek, under the thick dark of the willows and up the gravel path to the door where they studied the row of shoes at the doorstep. Uncle Kepa.

'Uncle Kepa.' The room was warm and beery and noisy as they hurried in to greet him.

As he approached the wharf gates he saw the boy look up and start towards him out of the dark. Then, strangely, he thought he heard the boy say his name.

He waited as the boy limped towards him, and then there was the boy's face under the light for him to see. And Christ! it was his own face. This was himself approaching. He held his breath. This was himself surely, at sixteen, going off to sea after the death of his grandmother, with some old clothes in a brown paper parcel. This was himself, broad cheeked, full lipped and dark, hair standing up like a kina, clutching his parcel to his side.

But no, this boy was smaller, more stooped, and he

dragged a slightly turned shoe over the footpath, down
the guttering and across the pot-holed road towards him.
Yet under the buttery light it was *his* face, his own
sixteen-year-old, young face. He heard his name again.

'Yes?'

'I've looked for you,' the boy said. 'There's no place
for me here, so I looked . . . .'

'My drop kick,' he breathed out of his past.

'I didn't know . . . so I looked. There isn't any
place . . . .' Kepa paused a moment then said, 'There is
a place,' and he took the parcel from the boy and
pushed it down into his swag.

'You didn't stay long,' Mereana said to Denny Boy. 'At
the party I mean.'

'Long enough,' he said.

'What did you do?'

'Me? Nothing.'

Uncle Kepa was pulling himself up out of the armchair. He staggered slightly and almost toppled. Denny
Boy and Charlotte stood and took an arm each. 'You
haven't ask me yet,' he said.

'But Charlotte did,' Denny Boy said to Mereana.
'Asked you what Uncle?'

'You haven't ask me yet . . . .'

'What did she do. What did Charlotte do?'

'Put a left hook on his jaw. He dropped like a bomb.'

'You haven't ask me yet, if I brought you a monkey.'

'A monkey!'

He stumbled towards the bedroom.

'Fell back on Geddy's fence and stabbed himself
before he hit the ground,' Charlotte said.

'In here. There my babies. Funny uncle . . . he found
you a monkey.' Then he showed them the boy asleep.

They were looking down at Uncle Kepa with all his

years taken off like old skins, and all the engine room grease and callouses and tight muscle removed by a reversal of time from hands and arms.

'Kip,' he said. 'My little one from Aussie.'

He lifted the blankets and got into bed beside the boy Kip, who moved only slightly. 'Funny uncle,' he said, then seemed immediately to be asleep.

Glossary

ake ake ake	for ever and ever
arohanui	much love
e hoa	friend
Haere ra e hoa ma.	Goodbye friends.
hoha	nuisance
kahawai	type of fish
kai	food
ka pai	good
ka pai ano	very good
Kare aku moni e tama ma.	I haven't any money boys.
kehua	ghost
Kei te haere korua?	Are you two going?
Kei te pai.	I'm well.
Kei te pehea korua?	How are you both?
Kei whea o korua hoa?	Where are your friends?
kina	sea egg
koura	crayfish
kumara	sweet potato
Kupe	Polynesian explorer
manuka	tea-tree
Mauria mai he paraoa.	Bring me some bread.
Mauria mai he riwai.	Bring me some potatoes.
Mauria mai he tarau, penei te kaita.	Bring me some trousers — this size.
Na te aha?	Why?
pakaru	broken
pakeha	European
paua	type of large shellfish

pipi	type of shellfish
porangi	demented
riwai	potato
Tamatea	phases of the moon
Tamatea Aio	when windy weather
Tamatea a Ngana	can be expected
Tamatea Whakapau	
Tangaroa	God of the Seas
tangi	time and custom of mourning for the dead
tarakihi	type of fish
tasi lua tolu fa	one two three four (Samoan)
tena koe	there you are (greeting to one person)
tutae	excrement
whakairo	carving (n.)
whanaunga	relative, blood relation
Whetu o te Moana	Star of the Sea